The song faded, and as Smokey Robinson began crooning "Ooh Baby, Baby," Jade threw her arms around Stevie's neck, her face cradling into the hollow of Stevie's shoulder, her hips still swaying, only slower this time.

"God, what a great song!" she breathed, nestling closer.

It took a moment for Stevie to digest her own surprise at Jade's bluntness. Finally, she let herself be pliant against Jade, luxuriating in the soft intertwining of their swaying bodies, the mingling of their scents. She squeezed her arms tighter around Jade's narrow waist, aware that only inches separated her yearning hands from that round, tight ass. But she held back, unsure of what Jade wanted, unsure of what she herself wanted. She knew what her body craved, but her heart recoiled in fear.

The warmth of the wine and candlelight, the expanse of the darkened waters outside, and the softness filling her arms began numbing Stevie into a pleasantness she hadn't known for so long, she couldn't remember when. She felt drunk with tranquillity.

Stevie closed her eyes as Martha Reeves and the Vandellas began singing "Love (Makes Me Do Foolish Things)." She didn't care if she ever opened her eyes again as she brushed her cheek against Jade's velvety hair. Soft, full lips glazed her neck in return.

"This is why I wanted you here," Jade whispered.

# Last Rites

The 1st Stevie Houston Mystery

## TRACEY RICHARDSON

THE NAIAD PRESS, INC.
1997

Printed in the United States of America on acid-free paper
First Edition

Editor: Lila Empson
Cover designer: Bonnie Liss (Phoenix Graphics)
Typesetter: Sandi Stancil


**Library of Congress Cataloging-in-Publication Data**

Richardson, Tracey, 1964 –
    Last rites : a Stevie Houston mystery / Tracey Richardson.
        p.        cm.
    ISBN 1-56280-164-3 (p)
    I. Title.
PS3568.I3195L37    1997
813'.54—dc21
                                                        96-45488
                                                             CIP

# Acknowledgments

This book would not have happened without the loving support and policing expertise of my partner, Sandra Green, who is my biggest fan, as I am hers.

Thanks to Dorothea, who is always there with her red pen and her blind confidence in me, and to Brenda, whose forensic expertise and keen mind I hope to draw upon heavilyin the future.

I am also thankful for the support and pleasant distractions of Beth, Lisa, Dave and Lisa, Julie, Chantel, Suzanne and Tammy, Pat and Heather, and Barb and Jan.

I thank Naiad for their generosity in helping me realize my goals, and my editor for her careful attention and suggestions.

And without my defective tonsils, I might never have sat down to this business of writing in the first place.

## About the Author

Tracey Richardson was born in 1964 in Windsor, Ontario. She is the author of *Northern Blue,* published by Naiad Press in 1996. Tracey also works the dreadful graveyard shift as a daily newspaper editor. Tracey and Sandra live in central Ontario's cottage country with their energetic Labrador retriever, Cleo.

# Prologue

He squirmed with delight, sweet sensation coursing the length of his body. The silk lace panties were soft and cool against his fevered skin. With each jerk of his hands, the metal clang of the handcuffs nipping at his wrists sent excited shivers through him.

He smiled up at his lover's face as the terry cloth belt was gently tightened around his neck. His bathrobe splayed out around him. He closed his eyes and waited for the lightheadedness, the disorientation, and, finally, the most electrifying of orgasms.

His heart pounded. He gasped and strained, wriggling with excitement. He loved the thrill of this new danger. His chest heaved with each conquered breath. The belt was tightened again, not so gently this time. The breaths came harder, less frequently. His head began swimming.

But something felt wrong, horribly wrong.

His eyes popped open, wide and wild with fear, bewilderment. *Why isn't he stopping? I can't breathe. By God, you've got to stop this.* His inner voice, the only one that could, screamed out. His hands jerked and flailed against the bedposts in a futile fight.

Pain throbbed from somewhere behind his eyes. *Help me.* His panicked eyes pleaded. *Stop this.* But his lover's eyes were narrowed, like a shark's, and they gleamed dark and evil. His smile crooked into a smirk.

*He's not going to stop. He's going to kill me.*

The awful recognition danced briefly in the priest's eyes before a gauze curtain swept across them. How many times had he counseled the sick and dying to be brave in the face of death, to let their faith guide them to eternity? Now the time for his own extreme unction had come. *Please, God.* He wasn't ready yet.

*God, no.* He wanted to cry, but no tears would come. *Forgive me, Father, for I have sinned . .*

Hundreds, no, thousands of times he'd heard those words as he presided, as God himself, in the confessional. Now those same words tumbled about in his mind, spinning, somersaulting, over and over, as death's shadow beckoned, as the echoes of his final pleas receded.

*Forgive me, Father . . .*

2

# CHAPTER ONE

The church and its surrounding buildings looked like a postcard as they sprang suddenly into view. The granite church and its attached rectory, built in the last century, sat thronelike on a grassy knoll, the perfectly manicured emerald-green lawn kneeling below like a faithful servant.

*So often the opulence of urban churches is lost in the shadows of the city's concrete, but not this church,* Stevie Houston mused as her unmarked police car wound its way up the drive, passing a sign proclaiming it to be St. Mary's Roman Catholic Church.

The church seemed to take an aloof pride in its standing, its power, with its panoramic view of the city below. Though raised a Protestant, Stevie felt a certain deference toward it.

*Prime Toronto land too,* she thought enviously, as she pulled the plain brown Chevrolet alongside the three marked patrol cars.

"The property alone must be worth over a million bucks," she calculated out loud.

"Mmm," grunted her disinterested partner, Ted Jovanowski.

A million dollars was hard to comprehend. Hell, she couldn't even afford the couple of hundred grand her Cabbagetown, three-story brownstone was worth. So, like many of the four million people in the Greater Toronto area, she rented at an exorbitant price.

"Just follow me," Jovanowski mumbled irritably, flicking his cigarette butt to the pavement as he unfolded his bulk from the passenger seat. From the trunk he retrieved a big black leather briefcase.

The veteran cop wasn't thrilled about holding the hand of a rookie detective. A woman at that. *A young woman, for crissakes!* How many men had ever made homicide by the age of thirty? *Probably none, unless he were the chief's left nut or the second coming of Christ himself.*

Jovanowski leaked a smirk, feeling big for his putdown of God in His own backyard. He'd been raised a good Catholic boy, being Polish and all. He'd even sat in this very church a couple of times. But church was a place you only went to at Christmas and Easter, or for the unavoidable baptism or wedding.

Religion, and the ubiquitous guilt it commanded, left a sour taste in Jovanowski's mouth. Maybe there was a heaven somewhere. He knew there was a hell. It was right here in the city — in the crack houses, in the back alleys, in the shambles of Regent Park, in the morgue. Purgatory didn't scare him. He'd stared it in the face most of his life.

A uniformed officer greeted them at the door of the rectory. Stevie didn't know the young man, but Jovanowski seemed to. A veteran like him knew just about every metro cop by now.

"Simpson," he nodded. "Is your sergeant around?"

"Inside, Detective. Second floor, first door on the right."

Without another word, Jovanowski strode through the door and headed toward the thickly carpeted stairs leading to the second floor and the private apartment of the parish priest.

"Houston," he said without bothering to look back over his shoulder. "When we're in, don't rush into anything, eh?" The words bounced off the walls with every step. "Take your time and look at everything. Smell everything. Let everything sink into your gut. Then write it all down. The stiff ain't goin' anywhere. And for crissakes, don't touch anything you don't have to."

He paused on the landing, more to catch his breath than anything else. He started up again, his weighty frame bobbing from side to side, the floorboards beneath the carpet groaning their displeasure.

Ted Jovanowski, Stevie'd heard and seen for herself in the three weeks she'd been partnered with him, could be as stubborn and about as tactful as a bull. He didn't take time for simple social graces. If you liked him, so what. If you didn't like him, it was all the same. But he was tenacious as hell and a good detective. Four years from retirement wasn't cementing his feet to the office floor any.

But Stevie knew he didn't care for her or, at least, he didn't seem to like her tagging along with him. He was assigned to be her coach officer because he was the best, and he tolerated her because it was his job to. But that was it. *Geez, it's going to be a long six months under his wing.*

"Sergeant Preston," Jovanowski barked at the officer standing outside the bedroom door. "Anything been touched?" came the thinly veiled accusation.

"Nope. Victim's inside the bedroom. We took a quick look, saw it wasn't natural causes, sealed it off, and called you."

"Who is our victim, Sergeant?" Stevie interrupted, pen and notebook poised. All they'd been told by dispatch was that the uniforms had called in a suspicious death at the rectory of St. Mary's.

"Father Gregory McCleary. He's the parish priest."

"Shitball." Jovanowski's thick lips curled into a scowl. From the briefcase he retrieved two packages of rubber gloves, passing one of them to Stevie.

"Ident been called?"

"On their way, Detective Jovanowski."

"Coroner?"

"Ditto."

"Any signs of forced entry anywhere?"

"Not that we could see," the sergeant shook his head.

Stevie surreptitiously slipped her hand into her coat pocket while the two conversed. With her thumb and forefinger, she quietly unscrewed the lid of the Vicks VapoRub container in her pocket. With a glob of it on her finger, she brought her hand up to her nose for a quick swipe, pretending to scratch her upper lip. She always carried the stuff with her, even when she had been on uniformed patrol, for just such an event.

Jovanowski wrinkled his nose. *Shit. Nothing gets by this guy.* He cast a disapproving glance at Stevie, his bushy gray eyebrows looming menacingly over his eyes. He let it pass.

"Where're your men, Preston?"

Stevie visibly flinched at the word *men.*

"I've got a couple out searching the grounds, and one's talking to the church secretary in the office downstairs, a Mrs. Powers. She's the one who found the body."

Jovanowski broke the seal on his package of rubber gloves and pulled them over his beefy hands. Stevie followed his cue.

The big detective opened the door, motioning for the sergeant to step inside as well.

The smell of death hadn't permeated the air yet. Fresh corpse, Stevie guessed.

"When did you get the call?" Jovanowski asked, barely glancing at the victim. He crooked a finger for the sergeant to follow as he slowly circled the perimeter of the room, starting at his left.

"An hour ago," Sergeant Preston replied, glancing at his watch, then peeking at his notes. "About one-fifteen P.M. We figure he expired overnight sometime."

Jovanowski glanced back at Stevie to make sure she was taking copious notes. She was. But she was chomping at the bit. Taking notes and watching

Jovanowski wasn't exactly high drama. She watched him peek underneath tables and scan the trim along the hardwood floor, all the while acting as if the corpse — and she for that matter — were invisible. Soon he was even crawling along the floor, his face inches from the rug.

Stevie's eyes were drawn to the victim across the room as Jovanowski continued his search. A middle-aged man with a thick shock of graying hair sat on the floor against a closet door, slumped over to the side. What looked like a terry cloth belt was tied in a slipknot around his neck and looped tightly to the doorknob. The dark blue robe he wore was open, exposing white, satin panties that almost matched the color of his skin. A magazine or book, she couldn't tell which, lay beside him.

Stevie wrote down her observations. The large room was in meticulous order, except for the bed, which had obviously been slept in. Nothing seemed broken or out of place. And everything was clean — not even a cigarette butt or a scrap of paper was lying around.

She sketched the scene. She'd fill in exact measurements later.

"Ted. What have we got?"

It was the coroner, Stevie recognized, watching him in conversation with Jovanowski. After a minute, they all converged at the cause of the Saturday afternoon disruption.

"Must've been some night," Jovanowski sighed before the body. Stevie stepped closer too.

"Looks like autoerotism," the coroner mumbled crankily as he peered closer. "Body's pale, face congested. Blood flow constricted at the neck."

Stevie's heart sagged a little. It was her first suspicious death since joining homicide. Like any keener, she was hoping to investigate a murder case, not a case of a guy who'd accidentally jerked himself to death.

"Priest, huh?" the coroner shook his head, whistling low. "He's dead all right, but I'm going to call in a pathologist. They might want to have a look at the scene."

With that he was gone, the simple job of declaring the victim dead over with. He wouldn't be the one performing the autopsy; the pathologist would. And no doubt he was calling one in case of religious and political problems with finding a priest dead from a bizarre sexual practice. He could wash his hands of it.

Stevie glanced at the magazine beside the body, then got down on her hands and knees to study it closer. It was opened to an article on autoerotism, with photographs demonstrating methods. With her pen carefully placed under the magazine's spine, she lifted it just enough to see its title, *Men in Bondage*.

She'd collect it later for evidence. Jovanowski had already drilled into her head not to move anything until photos had been taken and surfaces dusted for prints.

Her curiosity piqued, she knelt to study the priest's waist-high bookshelf that went nearly the length of the bedroom. There were numerous books on Catholicism, books of poetry, history, politics. Then the interesting stuff tucked in behind. Paperback fiction like *Long Leather Cord, Men on Men*, volumes 1 and 2; books on religion and homosexuality like *The Word Is Out* and *Holy Homosexuals*, and

9

several books on AIDS. There were a couple of books on S and M, the title of one, *Cuff Love,* prompting a smile from Stevie at the play on words.

She copied some of the books' titles into her notebook. *Well, well, a gay priest. What will the Church have to say about that?* She shook her head in amusement, remembering the tired old line she'd heard so many times: Hate the sin but love the sinner.

The bedroom was filling up. A couple more uniformed cops hovered by the door, talking with their sergeant, and a scenes-of-crime technician carrying a large suitcase had come in and was chatting with Jovanowski.

"Houston," Jovanowski returned his attention to her. "Go downstairs and interview the secretary. And check out his office, if he has one down there. I'll check out the other rooms up here."

Stevie balked, wanting to ask Jovanowski just what she should be looking for in the deceased's office. But Jovanowski had quickly strode off, as if reading her hesitancy. He wasn't about to hand her anything.

The middle-aged woman sat hunched in a wingback chair in the tiny office, which appeared to connect with a larger office. She frantically clutched a tissue, her fleshy face splotchy red and tearstained.

"Mrs. Powers." Stevie shook her hand. "I'm Detective Stephanie Houston. Do you mind if I ask you a few questions?"

Edna Powers nodded slightly, her featherlike hand barely acknowledging Stevie's.

"I'm sorry about Father McCleary," Stevie offered instinctively, her voice deep but gentle. "And I'm sorry you had to find him. Are you well enough to talk about it?"

The woman shrugged as another tear snaked down her cheek.

Stevie took the matching chair alongside Mrs. Powers, not wanting her five-foot, nine-inch athletic frame to tower over the distraught, diminutive woman. Dragging her chair closer, Stevie was careful to pull her open windbreaker across her body to shield her SIG Sauer .40 caliber pistol in its shoulder holster. Right now, she wanted to look like the next-door neighbor, not a cop. The fact that it was a Saturday and her choice to wear blue jeans, Dr. Martens, yellow rugby shirt, and dark green nylon windbreaker gave her the innocuous appearance of a college student.

"How long have you worked for Father McCleary, Mrs. Powers?" She'd start with the easy questions.

The woman sighed, taking what seemed like a full minute to focus on her answer. "Seven and a half years." She swiped at a tear.

"What kind of man was he, Mrs. Powers?"

She stifled a sob now, her chest rising and falling. "He was a wonderful man. He was always pleasant, always willing to help anyone. But this . . ." She looked down, unable to look Stevie in the eye, her hands clawing at the tissue. "I had no idea."

Stevie slowly exhaled through pursed lips. This wasn't going to be easy.

"Did he have any enemies, Mrs. Powers?"

"No, of course not."

"Were there a lot of comings and goings to his apartment? You know, overnight guests, or late-night guests?"

11

The woman looked hard at Stevie, her eyes pinched and defensive, her face hardening into a blank mask.

"I wouldn't know about such things."

"Did he have many close friends?" Stevie pushed on.

"I don't know," she answered sharply. She either didn't know much about his personal life or, if she did, she wasn't about to part with it.

Stevie eased off. "Did many people call on him here? Did he get a lot of phone calls?"

"Oh, yes," Mrs. Powers answered more softly now, a faint smile on her blanched lips. "He was very popular."

Stevie flipped to a fresh page in her notebook and steeled herself for the next step. This was always the worst part for the witness. In her eight-year police career, all of which until recent months had been spent in the uniform division, Stevie had seen the toughest of witnesses break down on the stand when recalling the details of a crime or accident they'd witnessed, or finding a body.

She leaned closer and dropped her voice to a near whisper. "Mrs. Powers, I know this is difficult, but I need for you to tell me exactly what happened this afternoon. Let's start with when you arrived."

The secretary squeezed her eyes shut for a moment, then fluttered them open. "I came here at about, let's see, one o'clock, I guess. Yes, because I made my husband his lunch at noon, and he always likes to eat right at noon, you see." She looked at Stevie skeptically. "Do you have a husband, Detective?"

"No, ma'am."

12

"Oh," she sniffed, her chin jutting out in judgment.

Stevie ignored the unspoken criticism. "Then what, Mrs. Powers?"

"I waited for him to finish, and I drove here."

"Do you always work here on Saturdays?"

"Father and I have an agreement. Saturday mornings, he prepares his sermons for Sunday masses, and I come in for an hour right after lunch to type them up for him."

Stevie nodded as she scribbled in her pad. "And what happened when you got here?"

She closed her eyes again, fresh tears staining her face. She chewed her lipsticked bottom lip. "There was no sign of his having been in the office, which is where he always does his writing. So I buzzed his apartment upstairs, but there was no answer. I even checked in the garage to see if his car was here, and it was. I felt, I don't know, strange, like maybe God was trying to tell me something. I knew something was wrong."

Stevie reached out to squeeze the woman's trembling hand. "You're doing fine, Mrs. Powers. Go on."

"I got the key to his apartment — he keeps an extra one taped to the underside of his desk for emergencies. But the main door to it was un-locked —"

"Have you ever used the key to go up there before?" Stevie interrupted.

The woman looked shocked, almost repulsed. "Oh, no, dear. No one was ever to go up to Father's apartment unless invited. He even did his own housecleaning."

"Are you sure the door was unlocked?"

"Oh, yes. I didn't have to use the key at all."

"And is that when you found him?"

"Yes," she nodded slowly. "I knocked on the bedroom door . . . and there was no answer, so I went in and . . ." Sobs cut her off as she hid her face in trembling hands.

Stevie let the woman cry a little, not wanting to rush her. After a minute or two, Stevie asked if she'd touched anything inside the bedroom.

Mrs. Powers shook her head no.

"Did you call police right away?"

A nod.

"Did you call anyone else?"

She stared at the floor before she answered, the red in her face deepening. "While I was waiting for the police, I called Father Chiarelli. I, I didn't know what to do." The pitch in her voice rose along with her breathing. "I thought he might —"

"Father Chiarelli?" Stevie interrupted impatiently.

"I'm sorry," she apologized as she visibly tried to calm herself. "He's the assistant pastor here. He lives in the apartment over the garage."

Stevie underlined his name in her notebook. "And he came over?"

"Yes. He made me wait here, and then he went upstairs to look for himself."

Stevie sighed in frustration. The more people who'd been traipsing through that room, the more likely it'd be contaminated with fibers, fingerprints, and God knows what. If, of course, this even was a crime scene.

"Was Father Chiarelli gone long?" Stevie asked the fidgeting secretary.

14

"No, just for a minute, though it seemed like hours before the police came."

"Did you or Father Chiarelli do anything else while you waited for the police?"

Mrs. Powers glanced at the floor again, sucking in her upper lip. "He, he went into Father McCleary's office and shut the door. I think he made a phone call, I'm not —"

"To whom?" Stevie snapped, not meaning to. Serious red flags were springing up.

"I don't know," came the flustered reply. "Afterward, he went back upstairs for a couple of minutes. Maybe he shouldn't have," she added quickly at the look of disapproval on Stevie's face.

Stevie reminded herself to breathe slowly and evenly. She knew better than to give anything away in her face or her mannerisms.

"It's okay, Mrs. Powers. Did you see Father Chiarelli when he came back down?"

"No, I just heard him. I'd gone to the front door to watch for the police."

"And when did you last see Father McCleary alive?" Another easy question to finish off the interview.

"When I left here yesterday at five o'clock." Stevie snapped her notebook shut and stood. She'd have to talk with Jovanowski about Father Chiarelli, see what he wanted to do with him.

"Thank you, Mrs. Powers, you've been very helpful. We may be calling on you again. In the meantime, I'd like to have a quick look inside Father McCleary's office."

\* \* \* \* \*

15

There was no sign of Jovanowski when Stevie slipped back into the bedroom. Only the scenes-of-crime technician from her department's forensic identification unit was there methodically going about his work, and a long-haired woman in blue jeans and Nike Airs was crouched over the corpse. A see-through plastic apron covered her from the knees up.

*What the —?* "Excuse me," Stevie challenged, striding quickly to the mystery woman. "Can I help you?"

Long-hair turned toward Stevie without getting up. "Well, it's about time. I hope you're one of the detectives."

Dark green eyes bore into Stevie, who inwardly recoiled in surprise. The woman at her knee was drop-dead gorgeous — smooth skin a full shade darker than her own, perfectly sculpted rising cheekbones, a long thin nose dipping to full dark lips, a wide, strong jaw. Her hair was as black as a moonless northern Ontario midnight. An Indian goddess — and a bitch.

"Who are you?" Stevie fumed, regaining her mental balance and summoning her own bitchiness.

Goddess-bitch slowly got to her feet, as though doing a huge favor, and Stevie was pleased to see that she came only to about the tip of her nose.

She didn't offer Stevie her latexed hand. "Forensic pathology. Jade Agawa-Garneau."

Stevie nodded sternly. "Detective Stephanie Houston."

"Okay, Tex, you want to help me get the body into a bag? Charlie said he's already taken all the pictures he needs, and I can pretty well do the rest back at the morgue."

Stevie frowned, annoyed by the unwelcome nickname — *Tex, for crissakes!* — and the fact that this cocky woman was telling her what to do as if she were some rookie constable. And where the hell was Jovanowski?

"Is it asphyxiation?" Stevie asked.

The doctor smirked, enjoying Stevie's novice clumsiness. "Is it murder, suicide, or accident, Detective?"

"Well, I wouldn't know," Stevie huffed.

"Exactly," Goddess-bitch rejoined.

"What about time of death," Stevie persisted, trying to regain control.

"If you'll help me I might be able to tell you."

Paper bags were already taped around the priest's hands. Stevie knew that would allow the pathologist to take fingernail scrapings — potential DNA evidence if there'd been a struggle. After carefully removing the terry cloth belt and sealing it in a plastic evidence bag, Jade summoned the photographer to take pictures of the deep red welt around the priest's neck. Then they carefully laid the hardening corpse on its side, still curled in a half-sitting position.

Retrieving a small tape recorder from the breast pocket of her flannel shirt, the pathologist quietly spoke into it, describing the advanced state of rigor mortis, the pooling of blood and fixed lividity on the underside of the legs and buttocks, the texture, color, and coolness of the skin.

"Okay, Tex, I'll be able to answer your question in a minute. The second question, that is."

Stevie rolled her eyes at *Tex,* and when she looked back, latexed hands were expertly inserting a thermometer into the corpse's rectum. Stevie quickly glanced away.

"Body temp eighty-nine point seven," she spoke into the recorder.

"Well well, Jade, you takin' him home now?" It was Jovanowski, a smile cratering his doughy face.

"Teddy," Goddess-bitch smiled at him across the room, tiny dimples at each corner transforming her face into one suddenly more youthful, soft. "I would, but he'd be a bit of a dud in the conversation department."

"Thought you liked the strong and silent type."

Irritation pounded inside Stevie's chest. *How come she's so pleasant to him — Mr. Sunshine himself?*

"I was just about to tell Tex your man's been dead about ten to twelve hours."

Jovanowski sucked the inside of his cheek. "Hmmm, Houston, Tex, yeah, has a certain ring to it."

Stevie sighed audibly, deflating the friendly banter. "When will you autopsy?"

Jade shrugged, her face stony again. "Monday morning. One of you will be there, I expect?"

Jovanowski nodded, still smiling. Christ, she'd never seen him smile like that before. *He even has teeth!*


"She sure is something, ain't she?" Jovanowski drew on a freshly lit cigarette as Stevie stared blankly through the windshield at the wet pavement ahead, the wipers chasing away lazy droplets.

Stevie shrugged, a scowl on her face. "Good

looking, yeah. But not much of a personality if you ask me."

Her partner chuckled. "C'mon, don't be catty now, Tex."

Stevie rolled her eyes. "I'm not being catty, and don't call me Tex."

"Oooh, the good doctor's sure pushed your buttons!"

"Look, she just doesn't like me much, okay? And I'd say it's pretty mutual."

Jovanowski chuckled, enjoying Stevie's pout. "I like Jade and —"

"Obviously."

"— and she'll like you too. You just have to get to know her. She likes giving rookies a hard time, is all. And once you realize you can't pull your superior detective shit with her, it'll be fine."

Jovanowski had seen enough rookie detectives in his time to know the pompousness was usually a cover for feelings of inadequacy. Not that he and pompousness were strangers — you just had to learn to save it for the right occasion.

Jovanowski smiled. "You gotta learn not to piss on these pathologists, Houston. They can save your bacon, or fry it, if they want. You don't want lab results rotting for months down at the forensic center. They want you to blow them, you blow them."

Stevie shook her head, both disgusted and amused by his last comment. Ice Queen probably wasn't meltable anyway.

* * * * *

The young priest stared intently at his folded hands on the table before him, waiting confidently for Stevie's next question. He was the picture of calmness, control, patience. The answers rolled quickly and effortlessly out of his tight, lipless little mouth. Not even one blond hair on his head was out of place.

"Father Chiarelli, Mrs. Powers said that after she called you, you went upstairs to Father McCleary's room. Did you go in or just peek inside the door?"

Leading questions, she reprimanded herself. It's just that this stony little weasel was irritating the shit out of her.

"Yes, Detective, I just looked in. Once I saw Father, I went back downstairs." He was emotionless, his eyes blank. Quite the opposite of Mrs. Powers earlier in the day.

Stevie closed her tired lids for a moment, wishing she was home with her mickey of imported Rebel Yell, her feet up, watching the Blue Jays on her thirty-inch television screen. Interviewing someone about as exciting as her shoe wasn't her idea of a fun Saturday night.

"And you did what?" she asked, boredom wilting her voice.

"I made a telephone call."

Stevie thought she saw a slight bob in his Adam's apple. A swallow. A tiny chink in the armor. "To whom?"

He hesitated, not wanting to answer her, this woman who dressed like a man. Brown hair cut short, parted on the side like a man's, her dark brown eyes impatient, power hungry, her jaw square

20

and strong, confrontational. But answering was the expected thing, the proper thing to do. He didn't want to end up in handcuffs. *She would enjoy that too much.*

"I called the auxiliary bishop who oversees this church. Bishop Kayson."

An eyebrow dipped. "Why?"

"The sudden death of a parish priest is a shock at best, Detective. There are things for the Church to consider, like the congregation, the transition to another priest, possible media leaks."

Stevie nodded, expelling full lungs. It seemed an odd thing to do the very minute after discovering the body of a colleague. She wished Jovanowski had come with her, but being the rookie and the fact that it was a Saturday night, the ball was in her glove. "Just talk to him, Houston," Jovanowski had advised. "It's not a murder yet, for crissakes. We just want to know what Chiarelli knows."

"How long did the call last?"

He stared at the ceiling as if calculating the exact time. "No more than two minutes."

"And then?"

"I went back upstairs. I thought I'd better check for sure that he was dead. You know, check for a pulse," he answered stiffly.

"You didn't think to do that the first time you saw Father McCleary in his room?"

Chiarelli swallowed more visibly this time. "No."

Stevie furiously scribbled on her note pad, hoping its effect was discomfiting. "Did you do anything else?"

"Of course not."

"Where were you Friday night, Father Chiarelli?"

"I was home all evening. In fact, I went to bed fairly early."

"Did you see or hear anything unusual near the rectory that night?"

"Of course not. I would have told you if I had."

Stevie delved right into Father McCleary's personal habits, hoping Chiarelli could shed some light on them. But like Mrs. Powers, he claimed to know little or nothing about his comings and goings, the company he kept.

"Suppose I told you Father McCleary was gay," she gambled.

A deep shade of red began invading his cheeks. "I wouldn't know what Father's sexual orientation is — was!"

Stevie waited, summoning every ounce of her waning patience.

His blue eyes blinked wildly, neck veins throbbing in tandem. "I can't imagine that he was a, a homosexual," he finally exploded, as if expelling something distasteful from his mouth. "Homosexual acts are intrinsically disordered! They are contrary to the natural laws of God and are not acceptable under any circumstances."

Ice-blue eyes lobbed darts at Stevie, leaving no doubt in her mind that this was also a personal attack.

"Homosexual acts are a grave depravity, the work of the devil!" he hissed, his chest expanding. He was almost shaking. "The only hope for homosexuals is absolute chastity, Detective. And a life of prayer and sacrifice."

His face began to lose its heat, and his mouth

relaxed, releasing its grip on the venomous tirade. He cleared his throat and his voice became more liquid. "The Vatican is very clear on that, and I'm sure Father McCleary would have done nothing to contradict the Church's teachings."

Stevie snapped her notebook shut, her heart still pounding in protest. She knew it would be unprofessional, and could even blow this case, to reply. She struggled to cap her geyserlike rage.

"Thank you for your time, Father Chiarelli. I'm sure I'll be in touch again."

She climbed into her car. Was it all right to feel such contempt for a priest? *Probably not, but what the hell . . .*

# CHAPTER TWO

Stevie cast a forlorn look at the wall clock: 11:10 A.M. The hand had crept only two minutes farther since the last time she'd looked for sympathy in its sterile face, the promise of escape still tauntingly distant.

Stevie hated attending autopsies. Her first, as a rookie traffic cop, had left her with nightmares for a week. She vividly recalled the initial horror of seeing a human body — pale, rubbery, naked — racked soldierlike on stainless steel. That first, overpowering smell of body fluids, formalin, and stale blood had never left her. But this was no memory. The Vicks in her nose couldn't mask the thick stench that made her eyes water and her breath catch in her throat.

*How the hell can people like this Jade whatever-her-name-is do this every day? Does she enjoy carving people up? Rats and fish in high school biology are one thing, but actual human bodies? Jesus, must be a bit of a nutcase to wanna do this shit.*

She kept her mind pulsing, working over her thoughts, even when they became stale or rambling. It was one way to keep from fleeing the room or dropping in a dizzying heap of unconsciousness.

"Tex, c'mon over here. Take a look at this."

Stevie groaned quietly. Was this woman ever going to quit calling her that stupid nickname? Why couldn't she just call her Detective Houston, or Stevie? *Hell, even Stephanie was better than Tex.*

Reluctantly, she stepped up and bent over the corpse, not really wanting to look at the dark red mush of the dissected neck.

"Can you see the bruising in the hyoid muscles?" Jade asked excitedly, pointing to a darker, magenta patch. Latexed fingers expertly parted the sea of muscles and vocal cords. "Just as I thought. The hyoid bone's fractured."

Stevie briefly scanned the sea-green eyes behind the protective goggles for a hint of derision, thinking the woman must be poking fun at her medical ignorance and distaste, trying to embarrass her. But there was a little glow in her eyes, a liveliness reminiscent of childlike discovery and the pride of a secret theory proved correct.

"Do you see, Detective, right here?"

Stevie nodded enthusiastically, not seeing a damn thing, just wanting it over with. And she didn't want to deflate what was the most animation this enigmatic doctor had exhibited so far.

Jade continued, her voice galvanized. "Remember earlier when I showed you the marks on his neck from the belt? The ligature indentation was thirty-five centimeters in circumference, whereas the neck itself is thirty-seven. That's two centimeters the belt cut in — a hell of a lot of pull, wouldn't you say?"

"What are you saying?" Stevie breathed, trying to rein in her own rising excitement.

"With his weight, and the distance from the door handle to his neck, combined with these injuries . . ." she trailed off, shaking her head.

"So it wasn't sexual asyphyxia?"

"If it was, I think he had some help," her eyes flashed.

Stevie's pulse quickened at the prospect of her first murder case. "That's great. I mean, that's incredible news. I'm going back to the office to tell Ted."

Jade threw her head back in spontaneous laughter, a scalpel gleaming in her right hand. "Whoa there, Tex, don't go galloping off into the sunset yet."

Stevie couldn't contain a tiny smile. It looked like she'd have to get used to this Tex business.

"You're not getting out of this so quick. Let's finish up, then we'll go back to my office and talk about it."

With that, her scalpeled hand deftly slid across

the cadaver's chest from the left shoulder to the right to start the typical Y-incision. Removal and examination of vital organs would follow.

Stevie exhaled in a pout, chin drooping onto her gowned chest.

Cradling the warm cup of coffee in her hands, Stevie leaned back in the wooden chair, glad to be away from the dead.

Jade Agawa-Garneau's office was small and antiseptic. Her desk was diminutive, veneer over cheap wood. Metal bookshelves filled with medical textbooks and journals lined the wall behind the desk. A couple of filing cabinets crammed one corner, and a tiny window looking out onto Grosvenor Street provided the only source of natural light. Obviously she didn't spend a lot of time in her office, and its size indicated she was one of several pathologists on staff for the Ontario Coroner's Office, probably one of the more junior.

"It looked so obviously like sexual asphyxia at the scene," Jade pondered, a slight look of puzzlement on her sharply chiseled, smooth face. "But the injuries are far too pronounced to be self-inflicted from a sitting position. He would have had to jump off a refrigerator or something."

Hundreds of deaths every year in North America were attributed to sexual asphyxia, many more than in previous decades when they were often labeled suicides. Jade was still fresh enough out of med school and her pathology residency to have studied the phenomenon, but it was rare enough that she'd only seen a couple of other cases.

"Typically, asphyxia is practiced during sex or masturbation," she explained to Stevie. "Some sort of ligature compressing the neck and cutting off oxygen to the brain supposedly heightens the pleasure of orgasm. On the brink of unconsciousness, the ligature is to be loosened, unless something goes wrong with the escape plan, as it sometimes does. But this case is more indicative of a hanging from some distance off the floor — or manual strangulation."

"What do you think happened?" Stevie asked anxiously.

"What, steal all your fun and solve your first murder case for you?" Jade grinned.

Stevie smiled timidly, glad for the thaw in their chilly relations. "That obvious, is it?"

Jade winked. "Not really. Ted told me you just joined homicide." Her eyes, unreadable now, scrutinized Stevie from behind the rim of her ceramic coffee mug. Stevie's thoughts felt naked before them.

"Maybe he killed himself and someone tried to cover it up," Stevie hypothesized out loud, remembering that both Chiarelli and Mrs. Powers had been in Father McCleary's bedroom before police arrived.

Jade firmly shook her head. "Sexual asphyxia's no trade-off for suicide. Certainly in the Church's eyes. Believe me, I do know the Catholic Church. And those marks on his wrists looked like handcuff rings to me. Couldn't have done that part himself."

Stevie nodded, lips pursed. "He was definitely into bondage, judging by his books." She remembered the magazine article on autoerotism conveniently opened. Could it have been planted by a murderer? "Do you think the body was moved?"

Jade swallowed a mouthful of coffee, unblinking eyes still on Stevie. "Anything's possible, but it would have been moved soon after death. Otherwise we would have known by the lividity. But yes, it could have been moved. There's no way of knowing where in that room the strangulation occurred."

Stevie's forehead wrinkled.

"The way the blood pools after it stops pumping through the body." Jade was feeling charitable, and something told her to be patient with this rookie detective. "Gravity will force the blood down, so if a corpse is found lying on its back for example, the blood should be pooled on the underside."

"Do you think that terry cloth belt was used, or something else?"

"The belt fits the markings on the neck, and I'd know by the markings if it'd been a rope or someone's hands."

Stevie took another sip and carefully watched the doctor's face for a reaction. "It appears Father McCleary was gay."

Jade simply looked at her, then slowly nodded. "I noticed the reading material too. And it was confirmed after my examination of the rectum."

"Any signs of recent sex?"

"I didn't find any sperm, and there was just a slight amount of seminal fluid on the underwear, though that was probably his own. Toxicology results will take a few days."

"So you're sure this couldn't have been sexual asphyxiation?" Stevie asked again.

Jade nodded, setting her cup down with a clink. "The injuries were far too traumatic for him to have died as we saw him."

Stevie stood, setting her empty mug down on the desk. "I'd say we've got some work to do."

Jade stood too. "You'll have my written report in a couple of days, but the lab tests" — she jerked her head toward the twenty-story building next door, home to the Center of Forensic Sciences — "will take a while."

"When will you be done with his robe and underwear?"

Jade tilted her head, appraising the anxious detective before her. It was kind of refreshing, even a little comical at times, to watch a rookie detective grapple with her first murder. Enthusiasm was no substitute for competency, but Jade's gut instinct told her this one had both.

"I'll tell you what," she smiled expansively. "I'll see if I can get the lab to give his clothing top priority. They'll search for fibers and anything else, though I doubt we'll be able to pull any fingerprints from it."

"Thanks," Stevie smiled tentatively, not quite sure what to make of the pathologist's transformation into someone actually likable. "I'll be in touch."

# CHAPTER THREE

Like a veteran quarterback, Jovanowski called out the plays, dividing tasks among himself, Stevie, and Martin Parker, a tired, wet rag of a detective a few months short of his sixtieth birthday and mandatory retirement. His energy and commitment to the job had drained from him years ago.

Inspector Jack McLemore had sighed apologetically when he offered Parker to Jovanowski. While Stevie was trying to hold her cookies in at the autopsy, a hit-and-run that killed an elderly babysitter and two small children had claimed a handful of homicide detectives, and a week-old gang-related shooting at a Chinese restaurant had the rest hopping. The Metropolitan Toronto Police Service wasn't exactly teeming with homicide detectives — just a little more than two dozen — because the city only averaged about sixty-five murders a year.

Parker's name had sent Jovanowski through the roof, to no avail. Still simmering an hour later, Jovanowski bellowed out orders as the three sat with McLemore in his office.

Stevie's return from the autopsy had kicked the department's crime lab into overtime processing latent prints and sifting through the evidence collected from the rectory. Stevie's job was to find out whatever she could about McCleary's background, while Parker would try to get the Church's records on Father Mark Chiarelli.

Jovanowski suddenly stopped his pacing and halted midsentence, the familiar pain squeezing his chest like a vise. He wheezed in shallow little breaths — deep breaths hurt too much — and absently backed himself into his chair.

"You okay, Ted?" the inspector asked worriedly, leaping up from his chair.

"Yeah, fine," Jovanowski managed weakly, the pain finally easing. This one had lasted a little longer than the others.

"You sure?" Stevie pressed, her hand finding his arm.

"Of course, I'm fine," he snapped, shaking her hand off as though it were a fly. "I'll go back to the scene tonight, see if there's anything we missed. I'll collect his appointment book and those porno books

32

you told me about and anything else I can find. We'll meet again tomorrow afternoon."


Taking dinner at her desk, Stevie munched on her vending-machine sandwich, unsure of what it was supposed to be — cardboard being the only discernible taste. She frowned at her watch: 7:02 P.M. Her eleven-hour day already felt like about fourteen, thanks to that grotesque autopsy.

She punched in the newspaper's telephone number and the proper extension.

"*Star* newsroom. Lisa Primeau here."

"Lisa," Stevie grinned into the receiver. "Stevie Houston."

A pause, then: "So, you finally came to your senses and want me back, eh?"

Stevie laughed. "Thought you'd given up by now."

"Never, my sexy gumshoe. Well, okay, I admit I did give up on you a couple months ago when I started dating my fitness instructor."

"Aha! So much for waiting for me."

"Hey, I'm still waiting. Just took a little time-out, but it's over now. My instructor moved on to another eager student. Sooo, what about it?"

Stevie shook her head, still smiling. She had to admire Lisa's persistence, which was probably what had led her into journalism. They'd met two years ago when Stevie pulled her over on the Gardiner Expressway for speeding. For almost a year after, Lisa had doggedly pursued her until finally Stevie relented. They dated heavily for about eight months until their relationship reached a crossroads. Lisa was too much of a good-time girl to settle down, and Stevie was too much of a loner, so Stevie did the sensible thing and Lisa still pretended to pine for her.

"Sorry to disappoint you, but that's not why I'm calling."

"Still too serious to get serious with anyone?"

"Something like that. Listen, can you do me a favor?"

"Anything for you, darlin'."

"Father Gregory McCleary, the parish priest at St. Mary's. He died over the weekend."

"I heard. Did you see the obit we ran today?"

"I did."

"What'd he die of anyway? The cops have told us diddly, as usual."

"Sorry, you know I can't tell you, and besides, we don't have the autopsy report back yet," Stevie half lied.

"But you're in homicide now, right? Does that mean he was murdered?"

Stevie tiredly massaged her right temple. She didn't want Lisa snooping about; she just wanted to get some information from her. She'd have to be very careful not to give anything away, or she'd have the shortest homicide career on record.

"Look, the uniforms just called us as a precaution, since he was a priest. I wondered, can you call up any past news stories on him with your fancy computers at work? Unofficially, of course."

"Yeah, I could do that. Tell you what. I just started my shift a couple of hours ago, but I'll be ready for a lunch break soon. Why don't I meet you at the Rainbow Café in about an hour?"

Stevie knew she looked like yesterday's soggy breakfast and quickly brushed her fingers through her short, brown hair as Lisa swooped into the café.

Swoop was right, for Lisa towered even above Stevie, her rail-like, lean figure making her seem even taller than her six feet, two inches. With that height, it was not surprising she'd headed to the U.S. on a basketball scholarship, getting her degree in journalism. A couple of years older than Stevie, she worked at Canada's largest daily newspaper, the *Toronto Star,* where she was a copy editor.

"Hey there," Lisa winked, bending over to give Stevie a quick hug, bracelets jangling and the faint smell of Obsession following her as she took the opposite seat. She set a thin leather attaché case on the floor beside her.

"Thanks for meeting me," Stevie smiled feebly, signaling a waitress. "An espresso and a regular coffee as strong as you've got," she ordered, remembering her ex's penchant.

"I must say, I've seen you on better days," Lisa winked again. Not a hair was out of place on her blond head; her clothes were perfectly pressed; her makeup was flawless yet subtle.

Stevie's smile was as limp as the rest of her. "Did you find anything out?"

Lisa glanced at her attaché case. "Of course. But not so quick, eh? How've you been?"

35

"Busy, can't you tell?"

Lisa appraised her again, not disagreeing. "Do you like homicide?"

Stevie winced. "Yes and no. I don't think my coach officer likes me much. And the hours! It's not like patrol, where you simply go home at the end of your shift."

Their cups arrived, and Lisa watched hungrily as Stevie attacked hers. Bedraggled as she was, the thirty-year-old rookie detective was still eye candy to Lisa — all muscles and firmness beneath the wrinkled clothes, her face strong yet youthful, the brown in her eyes rich like sweet dark chocolate.

"So, your priest," Lisa continued over the rim of her espresso. "I dug back through the national newspaper library system and printed out every story ever written on him in Canada. Quite an interesting fellow."

"Like what?" Stevie asked eagerly.

"It looks like he shone pretty early on, getting his own parish up north when he was still in his late twenties. But his star fell in a big hurry."

Stevie swallowed another warm mouthful, straining to concentrate on Lisa's words. "I'm listening."

"It seems he had an affair with an eighteen-year-old guy. The kid's father was pretty pissed, went public about it. Since the guy was eighteen, no charges were laid, but the old man wanted McCleary out of town, out of the priesthood, the whole shebang. Made threats too. Said if the Church didn't boot him, he'd personally see to it that McCleary never worked as a priest again."

"Hmmm, interesting."

"Isn't it though. It's all I can do not to run to a reporter with this. Anyway, the Church didn't boot him, just moved him to Montreal to work in the archbishop's office for a while, then finally gave him his own parish again in Ottawa. Must have been a good boy this time, because they moved him to Toronto three years ago, and he'd been doing quite well here, by the looks of things. Started up a street counseling service in the gay community downtown and did a lot of volunteer work with an AIDS hospice."

Stevie mentally kicked herself. She should have been familiar with McCleary's work in the gay community, but long hours at work and being closeted had kept her distanced.

"It seems he was really popular, and his church was one of the few in the city whose congregation was still growing at a steady rate."

Stevie nodded, lips pursed, eyes already moving to keep up with some silent train of thought. "Thanks, Lisa. I'm sure the Church wouldn't have volunteered all this, at least not without a warrant and days of red tape."

Lisa's voice dipped to a sultry whisper, her cheeks flushing. "Now that I've done something for you, how about doing something for me?"

Stevie shook her head, misreading Lisa's suggestiveness. "I've got no story to give you. Maybe one day, if this does develop into a story, we can give it to your paper first or something. But I'll be in the shitter if I make promises."

Lisa laughed, head back, long smooth neck exposed. "That's not what I was talking about, honey." She fixed hazel eyes on Stevie and licked her lips slowly, fully. "I'm done work at one. You going to be home?"

Now it was Stevie's turn to laugh. "Jesus, Primeau, you're still the horniest broad I've ever met."

Stevie didn't think it was possible to feel more dragged out than she'd felt the night before, but it was. Lisa had been her usual inexhaustible self, not leaving until 3:00 A.M.

Though the day had kept her busy at the diocese's downtown office gathering background information, Stevie's conscience pricked at her periodically. Regret tugged at her. She wished she hadn't relented to Lisa last night, taking a meaningless roll in the hay. What the hell was that all about? And why had it seemed like such a chore? Why was something always missing for her? Like a load of laundry on spin-dry, her thoughts somersaulted until she forcefully dismissed them.

The Catholic Church had purged any reference in Father Gregory McCleary's file to an indecorous liaison with a young man while stationed in the city of North Bay. There was simply no explanation for the young priest's sudden transfer south.

Stevie reported her findings to Jovanowski.

"Jesus Christ. You mean they just excised that whole chunk of his life from their files?"

"It appears so."

"Set up an interview with that auxiliary bishop and we'll tell him we know all about it."

They'd also want to talk to Bishop Anton Kayson to confirm Chiarelli's phone call to him after Father McCleary's body'd been discovered.

"Hey, Parker. What about our Father Chiarelli?"

"Clean," Parker answered in a disinterested voice rubbed raw from years of smoking cigars and drinking whiskey. "Church says he's a good boy. No record with us."

Jovanowski impatiently tapped his pen on the table, his voice barely controlled. "I want to know what he's like, Parker. Talk to people who know him, people he went to seminary with, whatever."

Stevie told them of her gut feelings about Chiarelli, how she felt he was hiding something, and of his almost violent reaction to homosexuality. The subject was obviously very personal to him.

"There's not much we can do without some hard evidence," Jovanowski grumbled. He hadn't come up with anything else at the scene they might have missed the first time. All they could do now was wait for the forensic results, something that left the beefy detective antsy.

His eyes darted to Stevie, his edginess evident in his flushed cheeks, the staccato of his voice, the pace of his commands. "Houston, track down this kid the priest had the affair with, and his father too. I'll start asking around the gay area, see what kind of friends he hung out with, what kind of shit McCleary was into when he wasn't being a priest."

Stevie's own face began to flush in anticipation. She knew she'd have a lot easier time in the gay district than a middle-aged, overweight, irritable, white male cop.

"Can I check out the district?"

Jovanowski eyeballed her. "What the hell do you know about the Church and Wellesley district?"

Stevie shrugged. Obviously her sexuality wasn't evident to Jovanowski, and she had no intention of enlightening him, at least not until she knew she could trust him. "I spent a year on patrol in Fifty-two Division."

Another long look, but he seemed to buy it. "All right, be my guest. I'd just as soon not have my crotch eyed by a bunch of fags all day long anyway. I'll check out the old boyfriend and his father."

Stevie sighed audibly. She was used to such blatant homophobia from her male coworkers, and every year her patience wore thinner.

Thickly carpeted hallways loomed in Stevie's semisleep, her head burrowing deeper into her pillow as she found herself retracing the familiar path to the library in her family home. The familiar mix of smells greeted her — leather books and wingback chairs, stale pipe smoke, fresh lemon Pledge — as her mind floated her into the roomy, hardwood-floored room. Oak bookshelves stretched the length of the ten-foot-high walls. Next to the window was a matching desk that once had seemed so huge, so intimidating next to her smallness.

On tiptoes, little Stephanie would reach up and stroke the soft leather books, all lined so perfectly, and inhale the leather and ink. There were law books (her father's), encyclopedias, history books, books on politics (conservative), books on economics, and the works of authors like Tolstoy, Frost, Kipling, Lawrence, Dickens (her mother's). Poets like Arnold, Eliot, Whitman, and Yeats graced the shelves too. When she was older, she sneaked in some Dickinson, Poe, Dostoyevsky.

Stevie smiled at the memories of the old books, but her smile, invisible in the dark, curled into a grimace as she remembered the finely polished table behind the large desk, and the one wall that wasn't covered in books. Family portraits, like toy soldiers, stood guard in glimmering rows. Frank Jr. grinning nearly life-sized in his graduation cap and gown, Julia with her movie-star smile looking tanned and triumphant by the pool. Pictures of them as babies too. Then more recently, portraits of Frank Jr., his wife, and their two happy young children. More pictures of Julia, her adoring husband, and new baby. Individual photos of the three grandchildren. Just one picture of Stevie stood in back of the table — her university graduation picture, small and dusty. None of her on the wall. Not one picture of her as a child. Her police college graduation portrait, which she'd sent them almost nine years ago, never made it to the family's wall of fame, nor any of her childhood softball or hockey photos. Too much a reminder of Sarah.

The last time she was home, three years ago, there were still no pictures of Sarah around. Not that she expected a sudden appearance. She'd gone to her mother's wardrobe closet when everyone was out, the way she'd done so many times before when she wanted to remember Sarah. Sure enough, wrapped in a box buried in the bottom drawer, were the old pictures of little Stephanie and Sarah. Their first birthday, their second, third, and fourth birthdays, dressed exactly alike the way parents do with identical twins. Their baptism. Their first day in kindergarten. Then nothing. About a year after Sarah died, the pictures of her, of the two of them together, had c0me down without explanation.

Stevie turned over in her bed, her eyes popping open, her stare frozen. She'd always wanted to ask her mother why Sarah wasn't allowed to exist in photos anymore. Why they couldn't talk about her. Why Stevie became so invisible after Sarah's death. But she never asked, because their faces were always closed all the time, their eyes distant, their mouths tight in a silent command for her to drop it. Her invisibility was what later prompted her to insist on being called Stevie instead of Stephanie, thinking the name change would cleanse her twinborn connection to Sarah, dead Sarah, in her family's eyes. But nothing worked.

*Okay, Stevie, so you come from a dysfunctional family like three hundred million others on this continent. So what else is new? They're assholes. Forget it. You don't need them. You don't need anyone.*

She sat up. A shot of Rebel Yell had her name on it right now. That'd do the trick, always did.

The phone rang as she padded naked toward the kitchen. It wasn't unusual to get calls in the night since she'd made detective. But sometimes, like right now, she wished she were still on patrol, where the shifts ended and began at prescribed hours. Rebel would have to wait.

"Houston here."

"Houston," Detective John Roulston barked from

the other end, not bothering to apologize, or even to sound regretful at possibly waking her up. "Thought I should let you know. Jovanowski's at Sunnybrook Hospital. Had a heart attack a couple hours ago."

"Is he all right?" Stevie was suddenly alert.

"He's in pretty rough shape. Don't know if he's going to make it."

"Shit. I better get down there to see him."

"Don't bother." Roulston sounded bored, like he'd already made the same call at least a dozen times. "Might as well wait 'til morning, nothing you can do anyway, except get in the way. Inspector said to tell you he wants to see you first thing. Says you and Jovanowski are the primaries on that dead priest case."

"Yeah, yeah," Stevie answered absently, cringing inside at all the work left to do on the case. A sickening knot gathered inside. What the hell was she to do now?

Stevie stopped at the nursing station in the cardiac care unit, already having passed several coworkers and a couple of patrol officers she didn't recognize. They all felt useless. Yet there was an inexplicable need to be there, to offer support to a fallen officer.

"No change," came the nurse's sterile reply. "Still critical, and he hasn't regained consciousness. I'm afraid only family is allowed in his room right now."

Stevie turned and sipped from the plastic Tim Horton's cup she'd carried in with her, not sure what to do. She and Jovanowski weren't exactly friends, but they had been partners for three and a half weeks. She knew she should feel *something*.

Stevie slumped into a plastic chair in the waiting area, still trying to label her ambiguous feelings. He was a good cop, she had to give him that, and he had to be a pretty good guy underneath. There were *some* people who seemed to like him, like that Dr. Agawa-Garneau. But dammit, he was so cranky all the time — and homophobic.

Wallowing in guilt for not really liking Jovanowski, Stevie didn't notice the long-haired woman approach her.

"Hello, Detective."

Stevie looked up, startled. "Dr. Agawa-Garneau." Stevie's mouth went dry. "He's not dead, is he?"

Jade laughed, her dark, shimmering hair falling back with her head. "No, no. You think that's why I'm here?"

Stevie nodded sheepishly.

"Look, first off, let's get rid of this formal nonsense. You call me Jade, and I'll call you Stephanie, capiche?"

"Stevie, please. Anyone who calls me Stephanie sounds like my mother. And Tex sounds so . . . redneck."

Jade nodded, smiling, and finally Stevie saw what it was about her that had attracted Jovanowski. The woman was persistent, brutally honest, reminding Stevie of a giant auger drilling and drilling until reaching the bottom of something. Jade's disarming tactics sprang from good intentions and a certain intolerance and impatience for the trivial.

Jade took the seat beside Stevie, her denimed

knee touching Stevie's, unnerving her a little, this invasion of her personal space.

"I wanted to check in on Teddy. But since you're here, the lab should be done with the clothing and bedsheets this afternoon. I'll let you know what they come up with."

"Thanks. I'd appreciate that."

"Hey, listen, I'm sorry about Teddy. He's a good guy, you know."

Stevie smiled in admiration of Jade's seeming ability to read her mind.

"You've known him for a while, I take it."

Jade nodded, immersed in her own thoughts. "He was the primary on my first forensic autopsy six years ago. We've done a few cases over the years, and he knows my husband fairly well."

Stevie's heart sagged at the word *husband*, irritated by the thought that this beautiful, intelligent woman should be wasted on a *husband*.

"Sorry, I meant ex-husband," Jade quickly corrected, again displaying her mind-reading adeptness, an exasperated laugh escaping her.

"Is that why your name's hyphenated?"

Jade frowned. "Please! Garneau comes from my father's side, he's French. And my mom's an Ojibwa, so I combined their last names."

"Cool," Stevie said, meaning it. She was beginning to like this woman. Though enjoying the little foray into personal territory, Stevie flipped back to her case. "You said something earlier about knowing the Catholic Church really well. Aren't you supposed to be given the last rites before you die?"

Jade, who'd been brought up Catholic and

attended Catholic schools, had no trouble summoning the doctrine that had been drummed into her over the years.

"It's called Viaticum. It involves prayer, anointing, and Holy Communion," she explained. "The priest prays over the sick or dying person and anoints them with holy oil. It's supposed to cleanse your soul of all its sins."

"But what if you die first?" From some reason, it bothered Stevie that this man should be cheated of the final sacrament.

"You're supposed to be given Viaticum before death. Oh, I thought you should know. Father McCleary had a visitor in the morgue."

# CHAPTER FOUR

"Listen, Stevie, this case is far too important to leave you on it alone."

Stevie nodded, her face clenched as tight as her balled fist nestled in her lap. With Jovanowski fighting for his life, she was pleading her case to be the lead primary on the McCleary murder. She didn't want to be reassigned or relegated to a tagalong.

But Inspector McLemore wasn't buying it.

"Stevie, I admire your perseverance and, frankly, I'd be concerned if you weren't in here asking to go ahead with this case. But let's face it. You're new at this and you need all the help you can get."

He leaned back in his chair, fingers laced behind his head. He was an immaculate dresser, especially for a cop. Cops and professors had to be the absolute worse dressers, Stevie thought distractedly. But not McLemore. His suits were expensive and custom cut, his ties fashionable and neatly worn, his hair trimmed exactly the same length week after week. His only detraction was the stale odor of cigarettes on his clothes and his yellowed, nicotined fingers.

McLemore's eyes darkened as he read the resistance on Stevie's face. Most rookie detectives had that smart-ass, lone-wolf attitude — it was what pushed cops into detective work. And usually if you gave them enough rope, they'd hang themselves. But this kid was smart and resourceful, a young female version of Jovanowski, which was why he'd plucked her from the fraud squad, where she'd only been for six months after having moved up from uniformed patrol. McLemore didn't want to see her career spiral like a kite caught in an air pocket.

"Trust me. This is for your own good. A lot of people thought I was nuts for bringing someone so fresh into this department, and I don't want to give them any ammunition. Parker will stay with you, and I'll be the lead. That means the two of you do all the legwork and report back to me. Let me call the shots. And as soon as Roulston is free, I'll move him to the case and he'll be your coach."

Stevie smiled thinly. She had every intention of cutting Parker out of the loop and doing this herself.

\* \* \* \* \*

Stevie sat on the park bench, flipping through her notebook while she waited. After her disappointing meeting with McLemore, she'd spent the morning trying to track down the young man McCleary had had an affair with in North Bay some twenty years ago.

Thanks to an aging North Bay police sergeant who remembered the original complaint, she discovered the angry father had died of cancer several years earlier. But the son, Jonathon Gant, was believed to be living in Toronto. A computer inquiry through CPIC (Canadian Police Information Center) showed he had no fixed address, which meant he probably lived on the streets and was fairly transient. He had a criminal record for petty theft and prostitution — nothing to get too excited about. But the fact that he did have a record, that he had a past with McCleary, and that he could still be living somewhere in Toronto, left Stevie exultant. Finally some tangibles to work with. The records department was trying to dig up a booking photo of Gant.

"Detective Houston?"

Stevie stood to shake the outstretched hand that was smooth and gentle, slightly tanned.

"Hello. You must be Father LaRoche."

Peter LaRoche looked about her own age, slightly built and a little shorter than Stevie. His neat light-brown hair and smooth face made him look more like a young banker than a priest, especially dressed as he was in casual slacks and a collarless shirt, a sweater draped lazily over his shoulder.

"Please, call me Peter." He smiled warmly.

*What a switch from Father Chiarelli.* Both were assistant priests for large parishes, but worlds apart

49

in manners and outlook, Stevie thought. She smiled back and indicated the bench. "Call me Stevie then, Peter. Or Stephanie if you want to be more formal."

"Stevie it is."

She nodded, already liking him. After waiting for him to sit first, Stevie sat beside him and plucked her notebook from the inside pocket of her cream-colored linen sports jacket.

"Thank you for meeting me, Peter. I'm sorry about Father McCleary's death. I understand you were quite close."

His smile twisted into a wince, thin eyebrows settling hard over inky, blue eyes. "Yes, we were. That's why I went and prayed over him in the morgue. I don't know what the men at the hospice will do without him now. We'll have to get by somehow, but it'll never be the same again."

"You worked at the AIDS hospice with him?"

"He was the one who convinced me to do some counseling and volunteer work there. One look at how much he was loved and respected, and I knew that's what I wanted to do too." His voice was quiet, like a night breeze.

For the first time in this four-day-old case, Stevie felt her emotions ballooning in her chest. She swallowed roughly, and it took her a minute to identify the sudden swell of anger at the violence of the crime, the regret of a life lost, the helplessness of knowing a killer was out there somewhere. For one who never cried in the presence of others, she suddenly felt the catch of tears in her throat.

"Did Father McCleary have any enemies or people who might have wanted to hurt him?" she asked, a tiny waver to her voice.

"It would be a shock to me if he had a single enemy, Stevie. Everyone liked him, as clichéd as that might sound."

Stevie nodded, regaining her composure. "How well do you know Father Mark Chiarelli?"

There was a slight hesitation, and the stiffening of the young priest's face and body didn't go unnoticed. "Father Chiarelli and I went to seminary together."

Stevie waited for him to elaborate, but he didn't. "And what kind of man is he?"

"It is not prudent of me to speak ill of anyone. But I will say that Father Chiarelli is ambitious. It has never been any secret that he aspires to be a bishop one day, maybe more."

"And how would he go about that?"

LaRoche shrugged. "First he would have to get a parish of his own. And quite simply, he would have to jump through certain political hoops within the archdiocese, make a real name for himself."

"Did Father McCleary have any such ambitions?"

"Not at all." LaRoche shook his head, his face pensive. "What mattered to Father Greg were people. Especially people in need. And it was that quality that gave him a strong voice within the archdiocese. He had the ear of the archbishop because of that special rapport he had with people. There have even been rumors that he was going to be made an auxiliary bishop."

"But, I thought you said he —"

LaRoche waved his hand dismissively. "I doubt he would have accepted, but who knows?"

Stevie contemplated as she scratched out notes. Was that pipeline to the upper echelons of the

Church, and possibly a promotion in the offing, enough to send Father Chiarelli into an envious, murderous rage? Stevie leaned closer to LaRoche, her eyes beseeching him to trust her. "Did Father McCleary have an agenda, or political motives of any kind, since he had the ear of the archbishop?"

LaRoche stared at his folded hands, a look of regret muddying his face. Then he raised his eyes, now blazing with pride. "He wanted the Roman Catholic Church to soften its stance on certain issues, to welcome and accept people of all kinds into its bosom and to love them all equally and unconditionally. He felt the dogma of the Church sometimes weighed it down, that it was essentially suffocating it. He wanted the Church to be more liberal, to enter a new era."

He looked down at his hands rather helplessly. "But it was difficult. There is a certain amount of resistance to such ideals." He looked at Stevie again and swallowed visibly, his mouth grim. "There is a certain faction, some powerful people, who would not want to see those things happen."

"Which side of the political fence did Auxiliary Bishop Kayson stand on?"

"Definitely the right."

Stevie understood his cryptic message, realized by the guarded look on his face that it was all he would say on the matter. And she knew Father Peter LaRoche believed in the same things Father McCleary had believed in, and that he would fight for those beliefs, just as Father McCleary had done, given the right opportunities. She wished there were more like him.

She spoke softly. "Peter, do you know of any relationships Father McCleary may have been involved in recently?"

She knew he understood what she was asking, and to her relief, the gentleness in his face told her he had been a true friend to Gregory McCleary.

"I'm not aware of any long-term relationships in Father Greg's past. It would be rather difficult in this profession."

"What about short-term relationships? People he might have been intimate with?"

Father LaRoche shifted uncomfortably and sighed. She knew it was a difficult topic, since priests were sworn to celibacy.

"Look, Stevie, I'll be honest with you." And she knew he would be. "Priests aren't perfect; they have faults and weaknesses just like every other human being. Father Greg did have a weakness of the flesh. But he was discreet about it. It wasn't something he flaunted, at least not that I've ever known."

"Thank you for that," Stevie said, touching his arm.

He touched her hand lightly, his eyes moistening again.

"Whatever anyone says, Father Greg was an incredible man."

Stevie picked up the phone on her crowded metal desk before the first ring ended, afraid it might be bad news about Jovanowski.

"Stevie?" It was Jade.

"Hello Doct —. Sorry, Jade."

"Glad I caught you. I've got some results for you. Can we get together as soon as possible?"

"Sure," Stevie shrugged, hoping the curiosity in her voice hadn't been too obvious.

"Dinner then, in an hour at the Village Bistro." She didn't wait for an answer.


It hadn't occurred to Stevie that Jade might be a dyke — her crowded brain hadn't considered it, hadn't wanted to explore the possibility. But the fact that she'd chosen to meet for dinner at a popular gay restaurant in Toronto's gay ghetto at Church and Wellesley, and particularly the fact that the staff knew her by name, sparked Stevie's suspicions.

Stevie took the envelope containing the autopsy report from her, and put it in her knapsack, knowing it was destined to be her bedtime reading tonight.

Over dinner on the busy patio, she listened to Jade explain that short blond hairs had been found on McCleary's bathrobe and bedsheets. Denim fibers as well. They weren't able to lift any fingerprints from the clothing. Stevie's own forensic ident department was at full throttle trying to match all the prints found in the bedroom, most of which appeared to belong to McCleary himself. Blood tests on McCleary and tests of other body fluids weren't ready yet. Fingernail scrapings were inconclusive as well.

"How's Jovanowski, have you heard?" Stevie finally remembered to ask.

"He's regained consciousness, but he's very weak.

54

The next forty-eight hours will be crucial." Jade's eyes, those turbulent pools of sea green, drank in Stevie's very thoughts.

*Her eyes are dangerous,* it suddenly occurred to Stevie. Their undercurrents were poised to suck her in, force her to surrender all her little secrets, all the dry, darkened corners of her soul that she'd never revealed to anyone before.

"How about you?" Jade whispered, leaning closer, her eyes demanding the truth. "How are you holding up?"

*Damn her.* Stevie sagged with invisible weight that burdened her shoulders. Her confident resolve was about to collapse in her lap. Though she was in the heart of an accepting community, sitting across from a woman she felt she could trust, Stevie nevertheless felt alone.

She felt as alone as she had that horrible afternoon when she was five, the afternoon her mother discovered Sarah facedown in the swimming pool. Little Stephanie had curled into a fetal position, alone and sobbing, as the ambulance crew, her mother, her older sister and brother, hovered over Sarah's limp body. Every night thereafter, Stephanie lay alone in bed, in the room she and Sarah once had shared, wondering what she had done wrong, wondering why she was so invisible to a family turned cold and aloof, wondering why she was so alone. Since that terrible day, a big part of her had become dormant.

Stevie felt soft fingers drawing a tiny circle on her wrist. She hadn't noticed the teardrop trickling its way down her face until it dripped off her chin. Embarrassed, she angrily wiped it away.

"It's okay. I understand," Jade offered soothingly.

Switching her thoughts, Stevie unloaded on Jade all her frustrations with the case and her growing fears. Could she, she wondered out loud, barely into her homicide career, solve this case? She had the textbook training, but did she have the focus and the necessary callousness to pull it off? And what if she became too callous, too insensitive to the victim and the violence?

Jade listened without interruption, wishing Stevie would say what else was bothering her. She told her not to be so hard on herself, that she could handle anything.

Stevie felt a twinge of hollowness in her gut as she walked back to her car in the darkness. She'd allowed someone a peek at the hidden parts of her psyche, had come so close to letting it all out. She felt strangely relieved, but at the same time horrified. What would be the next step, actually needing someone for crissakes? She shuddered at the thought.

Since her beeper hadn't gone off and there were no messages stored on her cellular car phone, Stevie proceeded with her next plan alone — finding Jonathon Gant. She knew she should have backup for her foray into what was popularly known in the city as Boys Town, but she'd been unable to get in touch with Martin Parker or her inspector to let them know what she was up to. She didn't want to wait another day. She wanted Gant now.

Parking on Grenville just east of Bay Street, Stevie slipped on her old blue-and-white leather University of Toronto jacket. She wriggled into her knapsack and pulled a black leather ball cap on her head, tilting the brim fashionably backward.

Her stride back along Grenville Street toward Surrey was confident but relaxed in this innocuous-looking neighborhood. Women's College Hospital loomed smack in the middle, while the safe confines of police headquarters were just a block to the south. Two blocks farther west was the provincial legislative building, its brown granite illuminated to a deep orange by night. Tourists, and probably many Torontonians, had no idea of the nightly fare offered here. This was Boys Town, where the services of boys and men could be bought by those so inclined. Women plied their trade a few blocks farther east, while transvestite hookers had their own TV Alley several blocks northeast.

Stevie felt eyes surveying her from the cars driving slowly past, and from the shadows.

"Hey, daddy. Whaddaya say?"

Stevie turned her head, her lip curving up in amusement at being mistaken for a man. The boy leaning against the brick wall couldn't have been more than sixteen, his hair cropped close, face pocked with acne, still too young to shave. When she got closer, she saw that his eyes had that opaque glaze common to prostitutes and street people high on drugs or just plain overdosed on life's ugliness.

"Hey," Stevie shrugged, trying to sound cool. "What's happenin'?"

Disappointment settled in his face at the sound of her voice and a closer look at her. "Sorry, thought you were somebody else."

Stevie smiled. "S'okay, bud. Actually, I'm lookin' for my brother. Maybe you know 'im?"

One denimed shoulder jerked a shrug.

"Name's Jonathon Gant." Eliciting no response,

Stevie dug out from her back pocket the picture the records department had given her that afternoon. Gant was unshaven. Dirty blond hair hung over his forehead, a star-shaped earring decorated his left earlobe, a mustache grew wild. Thick eyebrows left his blue eyes shadowed.

Again the boy shrugged. "Whaddaya want him for?"

"The bastard keeps borrowing money from me. You know, fifty bucks this month, a hundred bucks that month. If I don't get some of it back, I'll never make tuition for the fall, ya know?"

The boy leaned over the picture and sighed. "Looks like Snake. Haven't seen 'im in at least a week though."

"Snake?"

"He's got a tattoo of a snake on his arm."

"Do you know where he's staying?"

A lazy shrug. "Hangs out a lot with the shooters."

"Shooters?"

A youthful snicker. "Y'know, guys who shoot heroin all the time. There's a bunch of 'em. When they're not here workin', they hang at the White Palace in Chinatown."

Stevie smiled widely and fished a ten-dollar bill from her pocket. "Hey, thanks. If you see him, don't mention I was looking for him, eh? Or he'll take off and I'll never get my money."

# CHAPTER FIVE

Stevie paced her inspector's small office, her impatience coiled like a waiting cobra, as McLemore grunted into the telephone receiver.

After hanging up, he was quiet for a minute, steepling his yellowed fingers on his desktop. Then a half-smile.

"That was ident. They've got a hit on some fingerprints in McCleary's bedroom."

"And?" she practically shouted.

His smile mushroomed. "It's Gant all right."

Stevie's pent-up frustration exploded in a loud

exhale. Now they could raid the White Palace and arrest him for murder. Without solid evidence linking him to the crime scene, he would have been considered nothing more than a witness. Her mind whirled as she contemplated her first murder arrest.

"I think I know where Gant might be."

McLemore looked up, skepticism lining his face. An eyebrow crooked questioningly.

"A source on the street told me he hangs out with the junkies at the White Palace in Chinatown."

"The White Palace?"

"I checked with the drug squad. It's an abandoned storefront just off Spadina where the right password will get you just about any drug you want. But heroin is its specialty — the pure white stuff from China." Stevie resumed her pacing, eager to get on with it. "Our drug squad raids it a couple of times a year, but it never shuts down for long, apparently. Above the place is a bunch of rooms. It's more like a flophouse. Gant supposedly lives there."

McLemore stood. "All right, let's nail him. I'll get a raid arranged for tonight. In the meantime, we've still got to tighten the noose around him. We've got to place him with McCleary somehow. I want you to check out the gay bars, places they may have hung out together."

So preoccupied with doing the work of two detectives, Stevie hadn't had time yet to question people at the bars. She bit her lip, then pushed on. "I'll do that, sir, but I'd like to go along on this raid too."

Now it was McLemore's turn to pace. "Look, Stevie, you've got enough on your plate. If we bring him in, you'll have to be here for the interrogation, and that could take all night long."

"I know, sir, but I'd really like to be in on the arrest. It's important to me."

The inspector smiled reluctantly, his head shaking in resignation. Stevie was practically out the door as he gave her his blessing. "Good work, Houston." The door shut before he could get all of the words out.


The picture of Gant was getting dog-eared from Stevie constantly pulling it out of her pocket to show bartenders and bar patrons. She had a photo of McCleary too, and while many people in the gay ghetto were familiar with both men, none had ever seen them together.

Stevie's body ached from trudging through nearly a dozen gay bars, all of which were beginning to fill for a Thursday night of cruising or camaraderie. Her stomach was growling from the yummy smells wafting across the outdoor patios and onto the streets. She hadn't eaten yet.

Stevie was tempted to don rubber gloves as she descended grimy cement steps to The Vault, one of the city's seedier cruising joints. Looking around, she decided she'd rather cruise a park than this dingy place were she looking for anonymous sex. As its name implied, The Vault was at basement level and as dark and dank as a cellar. Tiny cubicles could be rented for ten bucks an hour. Another room was a theater for porn flicks; a chairless bar took up the rest of the space.

"You need somethin'?" the huge leather-clad bartender growled at her above the heavy drumbeats of rap music booming from the large speakers.

Pushing her unzipped jacket aside to show her badge, which she'd clipped to her belt loop, Stevie watched his face grow from initial annoyance to downright unpleasantness.

"Detective Stephanie Houston, Metro Toronto Police. I'd like to talk to you about something."

Glancing furtively around to ensure no one had heard her introduction, he jerked his thumb for her to follow him behind the bar and into a large walk-in closet.

He didn't ask her to sit down on one of the two wooden chairs beside the cracked, faded desk paved thick with papers. They both stood, he with his arms crossed impatiently, she with her thumbs hooked through her belt loops.

"Do you know anyone by the name of Jonathon Gant?"

He shook his head gruffly. "Names mean nothin' to me, lady."

"How about Father Gregory McCleary?"

He didn't bother answering, his unblinking eyes locked on her, brazenly hostile.

Stevie ignored his intimidation tactics. She'd seen them all before, and then some. She pulled out the ragged pictures of each man and held them up to his face, her voice as flat and as patient as the Trans Canada Highway. "Have you ever seen these men here, either separately or together?"

She knew what was running through his mind: If his patrons knew he was talking to a cop, they'd quit coming here in a hell of a hurry. The men who patronized this place didn't want to be found out.

Stevie slid the pictures back into her jacket pocket. "Look, buddy," she finally said, tired of the little standoff. "I've asked some simple questions. If your memory has failed you, my cop buddies and I will just have to start coming here for drinks after work. You know, in case you have a sudden memory flash."

She waited, crossing her own arms until he sighed and finally began to shift his feet.

"And another thing" — she was stoking the fire now, her voice escalating — "when was the last time the city health department was in here, huh?"

"All right, lady." His voice was audibly deflated, his eyes less steely. "They've been here. That guy you called McCleary was fairly regular here, twice a month maybe. The other one started coming here a couple months back. His hair was shorter though."

"Were they ever here at the same time?" A nod. "Did they seem to know each other?"

"I'd say they got to know each other pretty good. They'd rent a room together. The older one, he seemed to like the rough types."

Stevie felt like hugging the man. *Well, maybe not.* "Have you seen them here lately?"

He shook his head. "Not in a couple of weeks."

Climbing back into her car, Stevie glanced at the dashboard clock. *Shit!* She only had ten minutes to get to Spadina and Dundas for the scheduled raid at the White Palace.

Traffic, both pedestrian and vehicular, slowed her progress. Sometimes, though not often, Stevie longed for Calgary, the city of her youth. At least in that Alberta city, sprung from the surrounding wheat fields and oil pumps, there was the sense that in minutes you could be out of the concrete jungle and into the flats of the countryside. Not Toronto. Its streets and highways, like intricate veins, wound around miles of polyplike buildings that spread outward every decade, a cancerous tumor left untreated.

"Shit!" Stevie swore, glancing at the dashboard clock as she turned onto Spadina from College Street. She was now in Toronto's Chinatown, which was altogether like being in a different world. Restaurants and stores, their signs all in Chinese, went on for blocks. Wrinkled little Chinese women sat quietly outside by their funny-smelling meats and produce, reading Chinese newspapers and periodically glancing up at passersby.

Stevie parked behind the unmarked paddy wagon and jogged up to Inspector McLemore, who was waiting outside with a couple of detectives she recognized from the drug squad. Everyone was in plainclothes, all the vehicles unmarked. She could hear yelling from inside and knew she had arrived too late.

McLemore silently nodded his head in the direction of the front door. Stevie took his cue and entered the building, her pistol drawn. She followed the noise to the second floor, wary of the rickety stairs beneath her.

She was almost run down by a burly officer marching a grubby prisoner down the stairs. A quick glance told her it wasn't Gant. The second floor was a volcano of chaos, a trail of prone, cursing prisoners handcuffed and waiting to be hauled downstairs as the cops searched each room.

"Pat," Stevie called to the first officer she recognized, reholstering her gun. She'd known Pat Silliker, now a drug squad detective, since they'd gone to recruit together at the police college, and they still socialized a few times a year. Pat was one of just a handful of dyke cops Stevie was aware of, but they rarely spoke of their sexuality, and never when they were around other cops.

"Hey, Stevie, looks like you missed most of the fun," Pat smiled, her pistol trained on two squirming prisoners on the floor, their faces in mattresses black with dirt. "And watch where you step. Fucking needles all over the place."

"Did they brief you on Gant?"

"Yeah. He's a big fish in this cesspool, eh?"

"Any sign of him?"

Pat shook her head, her eyes never straying from her prisoners. "Nothing, and I think we're about done now. None of the little guppies here are talking much, but we'll keep on them."

"Hey, thanks. See ya around."

"You got it. Call me sometime."


Stevie's spirits had taken a nosedive by the time she got home; she was depressed at not finding Gant. She stared without focusing at the rusty-colored glass of bourbon snug in her clutch. *Maybe that little shitrat in Boys Town last night tipped Gant off that someone was looking for him. Or maybe Gant's just one lucky son of a bitch.*

But she'd get him. She was sure of it. She wanted nothing more than to put this case to bed and get that dirtbag off the street. They had the fingerprints, and a witness who'd seen them together recently. Once they found Gant, they'd get a warrant for a blood sample to compare his DNA with the hair samples found on McCleary's body and in his sheets.

Images of Jade suddenly pierced Stevie's mind as her tense muscles began to yield to the alcohol. Her eyes roamed through nothingness in the darkness of her living room as she remembered the tingling she'd felt on her wrist when Jade touched her over dinner last night. The spot on her skin had felt warm, ticklish, the feeling lingering the rest of the evening. But she'd simply shut off the tap when it came to thoughts of Jade — until now, the flow gushing so heavy she couldn't stem it.

Stevie raised her finger to her bottom lip and gently traced its outline. What would it be like to really be touched by Jade, she wondered, indulging in the fantasy of kissing that smooth neck, sweeping the silky, dark hair aside, and tracing it down her naked back. But it was hard to imagine herself with Jade, as a lover. She'd seen the way people looked at Jade when she walked into a room, how eyes were drawn to her as if by magnetic force. *She could have anyone.* The thought shattered Stevie's reverie, reminding her of her own aloneness.

Stevie blinked and finally noticed the insistent red dot on her answering machine. Swallowing another sip, she set the glass down and strode to the answering machine, hoping it wasn't someone from work.

She pushed the button. "Hi Tex. Sorry, Stevie."

Stevie smiled at the sound of Jade's voice.

"Listen, I need to see you. Don't worry, it's not an emergency, though it can't wait 'til next week either. Let's do dinner at my place tomorrow night. By the way, yes is the only option you have. You need a break from work, woman, and it *is* Friday night."

# CHAPTER SIX

Stevie cradled the bottles of wine in her left arm and pushed the buzzer to Jade's twentieth-floor penthouse apartment.

"Hi!" Jade's smile reached out and pulled Stevie in, along with the fresh smell of simmering pasta sauce and the violin strains of Mozart's Symphony no. 40 wafting through the open door.

Stevie beamed back, her nervousness lodging in her throat at the sight of this gorgeous woman. She couldn't peel her corneas off Jade, off the curve of those tight hips hugged by crisp blue Guess jeans, off the cream-colored silk shirt skimming over small, braless breasts. Her hair was pulled back into a solitary, shiny black braid that trailed down her back, giving center stage to her smooth, eternally tanned face.

Stevie felt all thumbs and thick-tongued as Jade took the bottles from her and set them on the island counter in the kitchen. "Sorry, Stevie, I should have told you what we were having so you wouldn't have to bring both red and white. Hope you like stuffed manicotti."

"Sounds great." Stevie smiled, remembering her manners. "Great place you've got."

"C'mon, I'll give you a quick tour."

She took Stevie by the hand to lead her into the sunken living room, reminding Stevie of the way children unguardedly hold hands until they reach the age when hand holding is supposed to mean something more than innocent affection. Was Jade's affection innocent? Was she like this with everyone, or was Stevie something special to her?

Unsure of what to do, of what it meant, Stevie slipped out of Jade's hand, the view from the floor-to-ceiling windows a handy distraction.

"Wow! What a great place to watch storms from!" Stevie enthused as she stepped closer to the view of Lake Ontario below her, the early evening's crayon streaks of pastel pink and yellow coloring the horizon.

Jade laughed. "Believe it or not, that's exactly why I chose this place. Not for the sunsets, but for the storms."

Stevie turned around, silently marveling at their common awe of thunderstorms. Her heart thudded in her chest as though protesting the small size of its cage, and she felt her warm palms slicken. She felt like a teenager on a first date. No, worse than that, because she didn't even know if this *was* a date, though it sure as hell was feeling like one.

Jade's smile and the flicker of amusement in her eyes told Stevie that her childish apprehension was transparent. Stevie mentally slapped herself. *Jesus, Houston, get it together!*

"C'mon, I'll show you the rest."

The spare bedroom had been turned into a den/office, complete with a pullout sofa bed, a home-entertainment center, and a computer with all the accoutrements.

Stevie's mouth was a desert as they stepped into the master bedroom. The floors were honey-colored pine, and the wood furniture was dark. A busy oak bookshelf filled the full height of the wall. The bed, a four-poster king-size monster, was stunning atop a thick circular Oriental rug. The pillowcases looked satin, and the stark multicolored quilt was cozy and inviting. Stevie swallowed hard, wishing she had the guts to scoop this woman up and onto that bed.

"Wow, it — it's gorgeous in here," she finally stammered.

Jade's smile was slightly mischievous. "I wish I had more time to spend in here."

*Me too,* Stevie thought devilishly.

Stevie filled the long-stemmed wineglasses with Châteauneuf-du-Pape as Jade served the stuffed manicotti, French bread, and garden salad.

"To you," Jade proclaimed, raising her glass.

"Me?"

Jade grinned. "I understand you broke the McCleary case. Congratulations!"

Stevie held her palm out. "It's a little early for that, doc. We haven't exactly got our man yet."

"Oh, you will. I'm sure of it."

Stevie reluctantly raised her glass for the toast.

"Tell me all about it."

They tucked into their meal and their wine, Stevie explaining how the evidence had come together and her theory that Gant, who'd slid into a career of crime and drug addiction since the affair with McCleary twenty years ago, had somehow blamed the priest for his shitty life.

"So do you think Father McCleary knew who Gant was when they reignited their affair this year?"

Stevie sipped from her third glass of wine. "Maybe. Maybe not. People's looks change a lot in twenty years, especially when you're talking about someone who was eighteen and is now thirty-eight."

"Hmmm. So Gant had sex with him a few times, got himself invited back to McCleary's place, got him into handcuffs under the guise of some kinky sex, then strangled him."

Stevie nodded. "He just wasn't smart enough to pull it off."

"Which is exactly why I know you'll get him."

Stevie restlessly drummed her fingers on the table, her eyes fixed on some invisible horizon. "I should be out there looking for him. He can't stay off the streets long."

Without a word, Jade strode to the stereo and abruptly put an end to the classical music. She popped another CD in and went back to Stevie. The thunderous drumbeats of that distinguishable Motown sound surprised Stevie from her introspection. The Four Tops were bellowing "Standing in the Shadows of Love," though not that Stevie would have known that.

Jade reached for her hand. "C'mon, enough about work. Time for some fun."

"But isn't the case what you wanted to talk to me about? Isn't that why I'm here?" She felt her words losing their battle with the music as Jade pulled her into the living room.

"As a matter of fact, no, that's not why you're here."

Without further explanation, Jade grabbed Stevie's hands and began pulling them to the beat of the music, her hips swaying rhythmically to each beat. "C'mon, don't you like Motown?"

Stevie tried to shrug as her hijacked arms reached in unknown directions. "I've never really listened to it before."

Jade laughed disapprovingly. "I'm not surprised. You Generation Xers don't know what good music is."

Now it was Stevie's turn to laugh. "All right, so I was still crawling when this stuff was big. But you weren't exactly an oldster at the time yourself."

Just for that, Jade twirled her around full circle. "Touché. But at least I was out of diapers. I'm telling you Stevie, there's nothing like a good Motown tune to make everything right in the world after a long day. You should try it sometime."

The song faded, and as Smokey Robinson began crooning "Ooh Baby, Baby," Jade threw her arms around Stevie's neck, her face cradling into the hollow of Stevie's shoulder, her hips still swaying, only slower this time.

"God, what a great song!" she breathed, nestling closer.

It took a moment for Stevie to digest her own surprise at Jade's bluntness. Finally, she let herself be pliant against Jade, luxuriating in the soft intertwining of their swaying bodies, the mingling of their scents. She squeezed her arms tighter around Jade's narrow waist, aware that only inches separated her yearning hands from that round, tight ass. But she held back, unsure of what Jade wanted, unsure of what she herself wanted. She knew what her body craved, but her heart recoiled in fear.

The warmth of the wine and candlelight, the expanse of the darkened waters outside, and the softness filling her arms began numbing Stevie into a pleasantness she hadn't known for so long, she couldn't remember when. She felt drunk with tranquillity.

Stevie closed her eyes as Martha Reeves and the Vandellas began singing "Love (Makes Me Do Foolish Things)." She didn't care if she ever opened her eyes again as she brushed her cheek against Jade's velvety hair. Soft, full lips glazed her neck in return.

"This is why I wanted you here," Jade whispered.

Holy shit, she was being seduced right here, right now, by a stunning woman who made her living carving up dead bodies! Stevie didn't know whether to laugh or panic and hightail it out of there.

Her hands were being pulled down to Jade's hips, then slowly guided to her ass. Lips met hers, gently at first, then more demanding, more insistent, with each labored breath. Jade's tongue pushed against

Stevie's timid mouth, their bodies still rocking back and forth as one to the music.

Still playing coy, Stevie parted her mouth only slightly, until the greedy hunter conquered its prey. Jade's tongue claimed its new territory, filling Stevie's mouth and leaving its wet signature. Eyes squeezed tight, Stevie staged a frontal assault, her tongue advancing for its own foreign occupation.

Stevie's hands circled Jade's thighs, caressing them lightly. Their bodies were clenched so tightly, only a crowbar could have torn them apart. Goose bumps tickled Stevie's body as Jade's lips clamped on to her neck, sucking, tugging, engraving its ownership until Stevie threw her head back in utter capitulation.

"I need you, Stevie, now!"

Stevie let Jade lead her to the bed she'd longed for just a short time before. Their bodies quickly became a sweaty ball of fumbling hands and half-discarded clothes, their heat electrifying the room and charging the air.

"I, I don't think I can do this," Stevie burst out, abruptly pushing herself up on her elbows, her lungs fighting for air. God, this was nothing like the hollow sex she'd had with Lisa the other night. This was something almost fathomless. She felt as though her feet were dangling, unable to touch bottom.

Jade's fingers halted their hasty exploration. "What is it, darling?"

Stevie closed her eyes, trying to escape the embarrassment. "I, I don't know, I —"

Jade gently straddled her, her hand delicately brushing the disheveled hair from Stevie's forehead. "It's okay. We don't have to do this if you're not

74

comfortable. I just want to know what I've done wrong."

Stevie felt helpless. How could she put into words her own insecurity, her fear of giving up control, of letting someone else pull her heartstrings? She was comfortable being alone. Letting someone else in like this felt like being burglarized, invaded. After all, the only other human being who had ever truly been a part of her, her twin sister, had abandoned her forever.

The tear trickling down Stevie's cheek was cut off by Jade's finger. "I've hurt you somehow. Can you forgive me?"

Stevie began to cry softly, not just for herself, but for Jade's selfless patience and understanding. She tried to roll onto her side in an attempt to bury her face in the sheets, but Jade would have none of it. Insistent hands held her face until her eyes were brave enough to meet Jade's.

"I don't know who's hurt you, Stevie, but I promise you right now, I will never hurt you. I will never do anything to make you unhappy. I think you're a very special woman, and I want to love you, if you'll just let me."

Stevie pulled Jade to her. She needed their hearts to connect, their bodies to meld together. She held on tightly.

Jade's hands resumed their quest for new territory, conquering the zipper of Stevie's jeans. Her fingers traced the hairline of Stevie's triangle, igniting a wildfire through the veins of both women. Stevie's tears subsided, though her lips cried out.

Jade's mouth enveloped Stevie's erect nipples, teasing them with flicks of her tongue, her hand simultaneously creeping down to Stevie's pulsating mound.

Stevie's head sank back into the plush pillow as she bit her lip. She had to rein herself in from screaming out how much she needed this woman — not just tonight, but possibly forever. Proficient hands found her opening and two fingers plunged in. Stevie's pelvis met the thrusts and thirstily devoured them, wanting more, wanting Jade's mouth on her.

As if reading her mind, Jade pulled Stevie's jeans off and obliged. Thrusting into Jade's eager mouth and incessant tongue, Stevie felt the stirrings of that first ripple from deep within her core, from within that private space that was so familiar and yet so remote. Soon, the ripple began mushrooming into a mighty wave, the sweet tide emanating outward, even to her clenched toes and fists, rocking her body into a quivering heap.

Without hesitation, Jade crawled up to her and held her tightly. "I'm here baby, I'm here for you."

Still breathless, still wordless, Stevie swallowed the fresh lump in her throat and held on, knowing this woman had just unleashed something in her that she'd never truly shared with anyone before. And there was no going back.

Jade's hand moved Stevie's to her breasts beneath the silk shirt that had been unbuttoned in their earlier, frantic play. Stevie let her guided hand massage a small, soft breast until she felt it respond. Pushing Jade's hand aside, and positioning herself on top, Stevie alternately stroked and sucked the quickly familiar, taut nipples as quiet moans grew more insistent beneath her. Stevie's sugary kisses trailed down Jade's belly, her tongue drawing circles around

Jade's belly button while her fingers fumbled with the button fly of Jade's jeans.

Some moments later Jade called to her. "You're wonderful, Stevie, do you know that?"

Searching Jade's serene face, her dark green eyes, Stevie could see no trace of the detached cynicism of one who studies death. Only calmness of spirit, and maybe . . . *no, no, no, it couldn't be.*

They hugged tightly. Whatever it was in Jade's eyes, there was nothing to suggest she was about to abandon Stevie. This was no one-night stand.

"Do you know when I first started falling for you?" Jade asked, grinning and moving alongside Stevie to caress her cheek.

Stevie shook her head.

"At the autopsy, when you tried to leave halfway through, and I wouldn't let you."

Stevie laughed. "I didn't know autopsies could be so romantic or I would have gone to more."

They both laughed until Stevie's pager, from somewhere on the floor beneath the heap of clothes, began rudely chirping.

"Shit," Stevie muttered as she reached for it. "Maybe they've found Gant," she added, quickly dialing Detective Roulston's cellular phone number from the bedside phone. The night table clock blinked 12:20 A.M.

Stevie said only a few words into the phone, but her tone told Jade it wasn't good news.

"What's up?" Jade asked as Stevie hung up and hastily gathered her clothes. "Did they find Gant?"

"They think maybe, from some identifying characteristics on file. There's a body in an alley, shot through the head."

"Christ. I'm sorry, Stevie."

"At least my case still gets closed. Are you on call tonight?"

Jade nodded. "Guess I may be joining you at the scene shortly."

Jade stood and went to Stevie, sliding into her arms and hugging her tightly. "Thank you for tonight."

Stevie pulled back to look into Jade's face. The tenderness was still there, still directed at her. Her instincts told her to shrink back, to run like hell. She kissed Jade on the lips quickly, then left.

# CHAPTER SEVEN

The curious milled about as if it were one in the afternoon, not one in the morning, all straining for a glimpse of the dead body.

Stevie flashed her identification to a uniformed officer and dashed under the yellow police tape, not bothering to feel disgust at the morbid appetite of the onlookers. In her early years in the traffic division, it used to sicken her to see the siren chasers turn out in droves with their video cameras and even their pajama-clad kids to ooh and ahh over a nasty car accident. Now it struck her as merely an annoyance, compared to all the other sick facets of humanity she'd since been privy to.

A wild kaleidoscope of swirling red orbs from the police cars slashed through the shadowed alley. A spotlight on a tripod illuminated the death scene, stark white light bathing the jeans-and-leather-jacketed supine corpse. What skin was visible — the face and hands — looked as bleached as freshly laundered sheets. The victim's head rested in a small patch of red made brighter crimson by the light, somehow not looking real, as if it were merely a Halloween gag. The metallic odor of blood hung in the air.

The body itself resembled the eye of a hurricane. Police forensic technicians scampered around the periphery of the body, taking pictures and gathering samples of blood from the pavement. Two plainclothes detectives and a couple of uniformed officers were searching the garbage-strewn alley for anything of interest — spent bullet cartridges, cigarette butts, dusty footprints that may have been left by the killer.

"Houston." Detective John Roulston emerged from the darkness. "I want you to take a look at this guy, see if you think it's Gant."

Roulston, a small and wiry man who looked closer to sixty than his actual age of fifty, joined Stevie at the body.

The victim was of medium height and build. His eyes were closed, and except for the blood beneath him, he looked as if he might just be sleeping off a good drunk. His hair was dirty blond. He had a mustache, about a three-day growth of beard, and a star-shaped earring in his left earlobe.

Pulling on rubber gloves, Stevie leaned over. With her right thumb, she carefully peeled an eyelid back.

"Certainly matches the description. Same build, hair and eye color, the star-shaped earring. Any idea if he has a tattoo of a snake on his left forearm?"

Roulston's glare was unforgiving. "How would I know? Until ident finishes with him and a pathologist gets here, we do nothin' with him."

Stevie nodded, silently taking her lumps. "Bullet to the head, huh?"

Another glare.

Stevie tried hard to suppress her irritation at the veteran detective's arrogance. His reputation was that of a good investigator, second only to Jovanowski in the department, but he was a hard-ass who probably wasn't expecting her to stay past her six-month probation.

"How long has he been here?"

Roulston shrugged. "Some drunk scrounging for garbage ran out yelling about a dead body a couple of hours ago. A passerby called us." He paused, his eyes squinting at Stevie's neck. "Geez, Houston, looks like I interrupted somethin'."

Stevie felt the warmth crawling up her face. *Shit, Jade must have left a hickey.* She cleared her throat. "Need any help here?"

Roulston smirked. "Look kid, if you wanna tag along, fine. But we don't need your help, got it?"

*Fuck you,* Stevie silently cursed. Instead, she mumbled her appreciation. Someday, she'd show them.

"Evening, John." It was Jade, still wearing the clothes she'd been in earlier, a denim jacket over her silk shirt. She benignly nodded Stevie's way, then opened a small suitcase she'd brought with her. From it she retrieved a pair of latex gloves and a plastic apron to keep blood and body fluids off her and to prevent her own clothing fibers from contaminating the corpse.

"Has he been pronounced yet?"

Roulston shook his head. "Coroner still hasn't shown up."

Jade scrutinized the body as she slipped into her protective wear. "You can call the coroner off. He's dead all right. Give me your sheet; I'll pronounce him."

Stevie watched as Jade signed a form on Roulston's clipboard, admiring her new lover's ability to command the scene. Death was her domain. And she didn't take any shit from anyone — she didn't even give them the opportunity. Stevie smiled, recalling their rather frigid first encounter almost exactly a week ago, then unknowingly grinned widely as she spun ahead to the evening they'd just spent together.

"Something funny, Houston?" Roulston wasn't amused.

Stevie coughed away her smile, knowing she couldn't dare look Jade's way right now.

Both detectives watched Jade examine what she could of the body without moving it, starting at the feet and moving up, all the while talking quietly and evenly into her tape recorder. She scanned the clothing for tears or bullet holes and paused at the neck to feel for early signs of rigor mortis. Carefully pulling the eyelids open, she examined the fixed pupils and noted their diameters, then gently turned the head from side to side.

"We've got an entry here," she said without turning to Stevie and Roulston, pointing to a bloody pencil-size hole just above and slightly behind the left ear.

Stevie crouched alongside Jade to take a closer look, the temptation to whisper in her ear almost too much. The subtle, familiar scent of Jade forced Stevie's eyes shut for just a second, half locked in delicious memory, half steeled in self-reproach. Both of them were here to work, not dally in childish romance, she reminded herself.

Jade's glance at Stevie was just a flash, but it was warm and full-bodied, as if she too were having a hard time keeping business from pleasure.

Roulston's head poked above, obstructing whatever silent communication was going on between them.

"We've got soot and tattooing here around the wound," Jade pointed. "I'd say the muzzle was one to four inches away when the gun was fired. And judging by the small size of this entry wound and the fact that there's no exit, it's probably a small caliber."

"Likely a .22 or .32," Roulston suggested matter-of-factly.

Jade turned and winked smugly. "Or a .25."

Stevie smiled. *Damn she's good!*

"I'd say what we have here is an execution, detectives. And probably by a left-handed killer, if the angle is from left to right as I suspect."

Stevie appraised Jade with nothing short of wonder.

"I don't see any signs of a struggle," Jade continued. "His knuckles are clean, no fresh scuffs on his boots. The killer was probably walking behind him, maybe even following for a couple of blocks. Once he got close, he pulled out his gun and simply fired."

Roulston pursed his thin lips and stood, his eyes skimming the horizon. "We're not finding much here." He sighed loudly as though dreading what he was about to say. "Any suggestions, Doc?" he finally asked, respect buried somewhere deep below.

Both women stood, Jade to answer his question and Stevie to watch the show.

"Well, John, I'd look farther afield, that is, if I were *you*." The intonation, strategically placed, made Roulston shift uncomfortably. "We've got a small-caliber wound here at close range. There's brain damage, likely some paralysis, but you know as well as I what shock can do to someone. He could have walked half a block like this before he dropped, not to mention he may have been followed for a while by the killer."

Roulston curtly nodded his acknowledgment. "When will you autopsy?"

Jade considered. "In a few hours. You'll be there?"

Roulston, who obviously didn't like the inferior role he'd been relegated to, snorted. "Don't have much of a choice there, now do I?"

A detective or uniformed officer was required to be present at the autopsy after a death under suspicious or criminal circumstances in order to maintain the chain of evidence. Otherwise, a sharp defense lawyer could point out that if the body, or a piece of evidence obtained from the body, had been left alone for even a few minutes, enough doubt could be created to suggest something had been tampered with or lost.

"I'll go," Stevie jumped in. Volunteering to attend an autopsy was definitely a first for her.

Jade winked. "Attagirl, Tex."

Roulston threw up his hands. "Fine, have a tea party. Listen, I'd like to print him right here. We need to know as soon as possible if this is Jonathon Gant."

"All right," Jade relented. "But I'll help you so nothing gets damaged."

Stevie knew she should feel relief that they'd positively identified the body as Gant's. But something tingled in her gut. It seemed an odd coincidence that Gant would end up dead a week after murdering Father McCleary. Roulston already had it pegged as a drug execution — that Gant was probably behind in his debts. But why would he turn up dead now when, by all indications, he'd been living on the streets and doing drugs for years?

Stevie watched the ceiling and inhaled her Vicks as Jade carefully fed a long wire probe into the bullet's entry wound.

"Bullet traversed from left to right, fifty-five-degree angle," she spoke into the microphone dangling from the ceiling.

Stevie turned away at the buzzing of the saw cutting through bone, seriously considering a sprint to the nearest sink. She was quickly regretting her earlier generosity, wishing she were home sleeping in.

She'd had the silly notion this might somehow be romantic, being with Jade. But the assault of sickly smells, the sight of the rigored, naked body, and the very live presence of Jade's pathology assistant prevented any leering looks or talk of romantic interludes. A few covertly exchanged winks didn't begin to make up for being in this god-awful room.

"We're al-l-lmost there," Jade said as she gently twisted the tiny forceps inside the excised area of brain tissue. "Ah, here's the little culprit." She triumphantly held the forceps up, the flattened bullet clamped within.

Stevie stepped up, her eyes avoiding the opened skull and exposed brain on the table below. ".22?"

Jade nodded. "We'll take some pictures and measurements, then it's all yours. And don't say I never give you anything."

Stevie laughed. "You're so kind." God, she was falling for this woman. What was even more remarkable was that this woman seemed to be falling for her too. A familiar dryness crept into Stevie's throat; an itch prickled her palms. She wanted to let herself go to Jade's loving arms, but she couldn't. Stevie, though fairly inexperienced in relationships, knew her fear of abandonment would hold her back from the possibility of being hurt again.

"You're not going to get sick on me, are you Stevie?"

Stevie smiled at the concern in Jade's eyes. "Nah! I'm getting to be an old hand at this."

"What is it then?"

*Christ, doesn't anything get past this woman?* Stevie quickly danced a mental jig. "I'm a little worried about closing the McCleary case. We've got

Gant's prints in the bedroom, but what if they were days old? Who's to say he was actually there that night, when we don't have any witnesses?"

Jade shrugged. "That's easy enough. Meet me here in a couple of hours and I'll do a microscopic comparison of his hair with the hairs we found on McCleary. We've got a sample of Gant's blood frozen, so we can DNA, but that'll take weeks."

With a lusty grin, Jade closed the laboratory door behind Stevie.

"Here?" Stevie mumbled anxiously as Jade planted a kiss on her lips.

"Why not? There's nobody around."

Stevie skirted around her and made for the table with the large comparison microscope. "Is this it?"

Jade sighed in obvious frustration at Stevie's coyness, or whatever the hell it was. This was one slippery lover.

Jade sat down and buried her face against the eyepiece, adjusting dials, her narrow brows heavy with concentration. In a lecture voice, Jade explained the morphological characteristics of hair — how the outer sheath was made up of tiny scales while the inner component consisted of a cortex, in which a central core, or medulla, was found.

"I've already compared the pigmentation of the cortex, and we've got a match. Right now, I'm counting the scales in both samples."

"And that should tell us?"

Jade was silent as she focused on the task at hand. Finally her braided head turned to Stevie, her eyes glassy from exhaustion. "Yup, matches perfectly. Or at least, scientifically speaking, the odds are forty-five hundred to one it's the same."

Stevie slowly expelled the air from her lungs. "Can you write a report for me?"

"Of course. See? Now you can put this case to bed."

Stevie chewed on her bottom lip. "Yeah, I guess so."

"What do you mean?" Jade asked, getting up.

"I don't know. There's something still bugging me about all of this, but I don't know what. I can't put my finger on it."

Jade nodded. "Maybe it's because you'll never know a definite motive."

"Maybe."

"Hey, wanna come over to my place tonight?" Jade reached out to caress Stevie's hand. "That bed of mine's going to be awfully lonely if you don't."

Stevie smiled at the memory of that bed and what they'd done in it. She intertwined her fingers with Jade's and swallowed the bitter lump forming in her throat. She should be jumping at Jade's offer as any other red-blooded Canadian dyke would. Hell, k. d. lang wouldn't refuse an offer like that. But her heart was wimping out.

"I, I'd love to Jade, but I really should wrap up the paperwork on the McCleary case so I can have it on McLemore's desk Monday morning."

"But it's Saturday night. Can't you work tomorrow?"

Stevie eased her hand back. "I really need to start tonight."

Jade slowly shook her head and crossed her arms

over her pounding chest. Her voice was low, her face grim. "I'm sensing an honesty problem here. Want to tell me about it?"

Stevie's laugh was nervous. "Are you a psychiatrist in your spare time or something?"

Jade wasn't smiling.

"Look, Jade, everything's fine. I can't relax until I get this paperwork out of the way. That's all."

Jade threw her palm up in surrender. "Okay, fine. Give me a call when you're more relaxed."

Stevie left with her tail between her legs, hating herself for not being able to confide in Jade, for not confronting her own hesitancy head-on. It was so damn hard. Pulling apart fighting drunks and chasing robbers was a cakewalk compared to touchy-feely stuff.

At home, Stevie threw her jacket on the floor on the way to the kitchen, and submersed her shame in a glass of bourbon. She managed to throw together a peanut butter and jelly sandwich for dinner.

The buzzing doorbell snatched her from her brooding.

"Hey, girl, you shouldn't be at home alone on a Saturday night."

It was Lisa, barging in nonchalantly as if Stevie's brownstone were still one of her regular stops.

Stevie rolled her eyes, hoping Lisa wasn't on another seduction mission. Because this time, it wasn't going to work.

"Just come in, why don't you," Stevie said icily.

Lisa ignored her and plucked a beer from the refrigerator.

"Listen, luv, I need to talk to you. But you look like you're halfway to a good piss-up, if you ask me."

"I didn't ask." Stevie sank into her leather recliner and reached for her drink.

"Sor-r-ry! A little testy tonight, are we?"

Stevie shot her ex-lover a shut-up glare.

"All right, all right," Lisa sighed, taking an opposite seat on the couch and pulling on her beer. "I'm just here because I thought I should tell you about the weird phone call I got at work last night."

Stevie's silence oozed her annoyance at this intrusion.

Lisa forged on. "Some guy called and started reaming me out about our paper not running the real story on that Father McCleary's death."

Stevie swallowed the burning mouthful, nearly choking, and leaned forward, her senses quickly sharpening.

"What'd he say?"

"He told me McCleary was a pervert and a fag, and that he strangled himself while jerking off. Don't they call that autoerotism, or breathless love or something? I think I saw it on the Oprah —"

"What else did he say?"

"That was it. He said our paper was trash because we ran an obit saying what a good guy he was, when he was really some raging perv. Said he deserved to die like that."

"Holy shit," Stevie murmured, rubbing sobriety back into her temples. "Nobody knows that stuff except cops and the coroner's office."

"That's really how he died?"

"Something like that. Listen, when did this guy call?"

"Just after midnight. I remember because we were just putting the first Saturday edition to bed when he called."

"He didn't say anything else?"

"No."

"Did he identify himself?"

"No, of course not. Cowards never do."

"Was there anything distinctive about his voice?"

Lisa thought for a moment. "No, but he didn't use trashy words, you know? He sounded educated. Jesus, I feel like I'm being interrogated."

"You are. And I'm going to need you to come into the office sometime for a sworn statement."

"Ah, c'mon, Stevie. You know how journalists feel about getting involved in stuff like this." She licked her finger and slowly circled the lip of the bottle, then leaned forward, mischief dancing in her eyes. "Can't you just take my *oral* statement right here, if you know what I mean."

Stevie frowned, her voice like sizzling fried bacon. "No. I told you, no more of that."

"All right, all right. Can't blame a girl for trying. Say, what's with the long face tonight anyway? We should go out to the bars, cruise for girlies."

"Forget it. I've got everything I need right here." Stevie pointed to the half-empty bottle on the floor.

Lisa took another swallow of beer. "So what's the matter with you anyway?"

Stevie shrugged.

"Trouble in the love department maybe?"

When Stevie didn't answer, Lisa grinned victoriously. "I knew it! So you've met someone?"

Another shrug. "Maybe."

"Maybe nothin'. You have, you dog, you. So is it love, or is it just sex?"

"Geez, Primeau, you're like some hag who can't get enough of her own, sucking up crumbs from other people's love lives."

Refusing to be insulted, Lisa was still beaming. "Whatever. So tell me about her!"

Stevie loudly exhaled, a hesitant smile sweeping her face. "She's pretty great."

"Why aren't you with her right now?"

Stevie took another sip, then tipped more into her empty glass. "I don't know. You know me, you said it once yourself, about me being too serious to get serious with anyone."

Lisa slowly nodded, her grin fading. That was her Stevie all right, too afraid to give herself fully to anyone, Lisa knew from experience. Setting her empty beer bottle down, Lisa moved to the leather ottoman in front of Stevie and sat down.

"Listen to me, Stevie. One of these days, you're going to have to quit giving in to your fears, or you're going to end up alone. Is this what you want to be doing, sitting here alone with a bottle every weekend?"

Stevie had to shake her head to be sure she was hearing what she thought she was hearing. Seeing Lisa waxing serious was about as rare as seeing an alligator march down Yonge Street, and that wasn't about to happen anytime soon.

"I mean it, Stevie. If she's as great as you say, then don't be stupid."

Stevie reached for Lisa's hand, appreciating the heartfelt advice. Perhaps she'd underestimated her old girlfriend. "You're all right, you know that, Primeau?"

"Yeah, well, you're not exactly chopped liver either, Houston."

It was when Stevie was showing Lisa out that she noticed her jacket on the floor. Picking it up, she spotted the unfamiliar cassette tape that had fallen beneath it.

She slid it into the cassette deck and punched the buttons, curious. When the drumbeats started and Martha Reeves and the Vandellas began admonishing "Nowhere to Run to, Nowhere to Hide," Stevie burst out laughing until her gut hurt. Then she cried until her whole body hurt.

# CHAPTER EIGHT

Stevie gazed sleepily at the profile of the woman lying next to her — the finely chiseled nose, the lips curled down in repose, the eyelids peacefully shutting out the world. She smiled in the dusky light, admiration filling her heart with a prickly giddiness she'd never felt before.

*So this is what it feels like,* she thought with amused detachment. She remembered her cold cynicism, that love was some kind of mirage, an empty promise. She had never felt deprived, or that love had left her an orphan, for she had always considered love an illusion. Now, for the first time, she knew there was a kind of love to die for and a person in her life to live for.

She'd gone straight to Jade's after listening to that silly Motown tape, after she'd wrung her body out from crying. Lisa had been right. She was being stupid trying to squeeze Jade out of her heart for fear of abandonment. So she'd told Jade everything, including the most painful memories of her sister's death and the aftermath, her family's aloofness, and of her subsequent fears of getting close to anyone. All through it, Jade had held and caressed her, listening without interruption. Jade had been relieved to learn the reason behind Stevie's skittishness, and well into the early morning hours, they finally made long, gentle love.

Jade stirred beside her, her subconscious sensing a pair of staring eyes. She smiled groggily and rolled over, pressing her naked body into Stevie.

"It's so nice to wake up next to you," Jade breathed into Stevie's neck. "I want to wake up every morning like this."

"Mmm, me too."

"Move in with me."

Stevie pulled back and eyed Jade carefully. "Already? Just like that?"

Jade's laugh was meant to scold. "Yes, just like that. You're not getting cold feet on me again, are you?"

Stevie smiled in capitulation. "No. It's just, you don't even know all my irritating little habits yet."

Jade snuggled back into her. "I don't care, I'll take you, warts and all. I know how my heart feels, and it wants you here."

Stevie squeezed back, knowing that her halfhearted attempt at pragmatism was futile. "All right, all right, we'll move in together. Just let me get this McCleary case wrapped up. Until then, I can't even begin to think about packing and — "

"Whoa there," Jade cut her off, propping herself up on her elbow, her face souring. "I thought the case *was* closed, now that we can put Gant at the scene."

Stevie winced as she rolled onto her back. "Someone called the *Toronto Star* early Saturday morning and gave some details about how McCleary died — details no one but the killer, or those who saw the body, should know."

Jade frowned her confusion. "Maybe it was Gant who called, right before he was killed."

Stevie shook her head. "No, the call was definitely after midnight. And Gant was dead by midnight."

"C'mon, let's go." Jade scrambled out of bed.

"Go where?"

"To see someone who just might be able to help us out."

The door to room 207 was already open, but Jade, leading the way, knocked briskly a couple of times before trooping in.

Jovanowski lay in the hospital bed, propped up at a 45-degree angle, his large body leaving little room between the metal rails on either side. To Jade's discriminating eye, he looked as though he'd shed at least a dozen pounds. His pale skin was doughy and hung loosely on him, but at least he was alive.

A kiss on his cheek from Jade sent his eyelids groggily open. A brief, almost pained smile crossed his blanched lips as recognition rippled across his eyes.

"How are you, Teddy? We've been worried about you."

Another brief smile. "Just thought I'd take a little time out," he whispered, his slow and deliberate words robbed of humor. "Had a little vacation time owing to me."

Stevie stepped up to the bedside, unsure of whether to touch his hand or kiss him or what. So she simply stood, soaking up the silence until her discomfort began to wane. "We miss you at the office, Ted."

He limply waved his right hand, barely lifting it off the bed. "You don't need me, kid. You're already off and running, I hear."

Stevie smiled at the unexpected compliment. Perhaps seeing his life flash before his eyes had turned him into a soft touch. Or maybe he'd been one all along.

"That's not true," Stevie smiled.

Jade was studying his chart at the foot of the bed. "Looks like you've had a pretty rough go of it, Ted. But you've made it this far. You'll be okay now. It'll just take you a while to get back on your feet."

Jovanowski turned his head away, his battleship-gray eyes unblinking, heavy with thoughts he wasn't about to share.

Stevie and Jade exchanged knowing glances. They'd come because they could use the veteran detective's insight and instinct. But they also realized their need would give him the mental boost that could make or break his recovery at this crucial junction.

They noisily pulled the only two chairs in the room up to the bed.

Jade cleared her throat and nodded at Stevie.

"Ted, I need to talk to you about the McCleary case."

Stevie waited until he turned his eyes to her — eyes as dull and lifeless as an overcast November day. It wasn't difficult to conclude that the big man before her had all but given up on life — the feisty perfectionist in him having ebbed away with every struggling beat of his defective heart.

Slowly, Stevie explained how, just when the evidence against Gant had all come together, he was found murdered. And while that should have sealed the McCleary case, her editor friend had received a mysterious phone call from someone who knew intimate details of the priest's death. Not only that, but this person had a passionate dislike for Father McCleary.

"Maybe McCleary wasn't well liked. Maybe he had a few enemies," Jovanowski answered hoarsely.

"But that's just it, he *was* well liked." Stevie described her meeting with the young Father Peter LaRoche, his explanation of Father McCleary's much-admired work in the gay community and the AIDS community, and how his liberal thinking was gaining respect within the archdiocese.

Jovanowski motioned for a drink of water, and Jade obliged. Both women noticed the tiny transformation in his eyes — the small flicker of animation.

"So we know Gant didn't like him. Who else?"

Stevie shrugged.

"Look, Stevie, I know what the Catholic Church is like. So do you, Jade." His voice was gaining strength, the timbre deep again, the usual caustic edge seeping back in. Shades of the old Jovanowski were coloring their way back into the man before them.

"If he was left-wing, he couldn't have had the respect of everyone in the archdiocese," Jovanowski continued. "Catholicism is like a dinosaur. It hasn't changed much over the centuries."

Jade nodded. "He's right about that. A lot of people who hold power positions within the Church would view any change as a real threat, both to their own power base, and to the Church itself."

Stevie whistled quietly, grasping the mental picture being painted before her. "We need to find who might have felt threatened by McCleary. But what does that have to do with Gant?"

Jovanowski pondered her question, the wrinkles in his forehead straining until they resembled a well-traveled roadmap. "You got me on that one. Unless Gant was hired to be the killer."

Stevie felt as though her heart would gallop away on her. This was getting awfully big in a hurry. If it was true, she was in way over her head with this case. "It meant someone had to have known about McCleary's history with Gant."

"The Church certainly knew," Jovanowski offered.

"And so Gant would have started up this recent affair in order to set up the killing," Stevie thought out loud. "Do you think this same person, this mastermind or whatever, had Gant killed as well?"

Jovanowski shrugged. "If Gant was hired to kill

McCleary, it would make sense to blow him away. A drug addict like him couldn't be trusted to keep his mouth shut."

Stevie didn't like the feel of this one bit, if indeed any of these hypotheses could be believed. They implied evil, a deeply rooted cancer within the Church. "So you're saying you don't buy the idea that Gant offed McCleary as a form of revenge for screwing up his life?"

Jovanowski smirked. "No way. Why would he go to all that trouble if there weren't something in it for him? I know guys like that, Stevie, druggies who live off the street. They don't do nothin' unless there's cash or some drug fix in it for them. I mean, for crissakes, he didn't even steal anything from McCleary's place."

Stevie shook her head. "Look, Ted, I don't know. There's no way I'm going to convince McLemore or anyone else at headquarters of our theory. As far as they're concerned, the case is closed."

"Maybe not." Jade tried to sound hopeful. "They don't know about the phone call to your friend."

Stevie shook her head again. "They won't go for it. And I'd be way out of my league anyway."

A hint of a smile cracked Jovanowski's face, the glow of mischief in his eyes. But his voice was serious. "You're right, kid. You couldn't handle it anyway. Just forget about it. Maybe someday if I ever get out of here, we'll look into it again."

Stevie crossed her arms over her chest to suppress her rising anger. Was anyone in her own department ever going to treat her like an equal? Or was she forever going to be the kid, the rookie detective?

She inhaled deeply, then let her breath out slowly.

There was no point in getting Jovanowski all worked up by throwing a temper tantrum. They'd worked him over enough today as it was. "All right. Suppose McLemore did give me a bit of rope with this. Where would I start?"

Jovanowski smothered a smile. His student had taken the bait. "You'd start with who you know for sure didn't agree with McCleary's views."

Stevie thought for a moment. "Father Mark Chiarelli?"

Jovanowski nodded triumphantly. "You said he had a real attitude problem."

Stevie stood, eager for a long walk or a jog so she could chew on everything they'd discussed, and then some. She knew she'd be wading into some pretty turbulent waters ahead, and it would take some slow and deliberate navigation to get through them. A little luck wouldn't hurt either.

"Hey, since when did you two get to bein' friends?" The observation had just struck Jovanowski.

Jade grinned and aimed a wink at Jovanowski. "Tex is okay, Teddy. She's okay."

Inspector McLemore listened as Stevie expounded her theory, but his bland expression implied he was simply humoring her.

Finally, he'd had enough, the last grain of his patience having washed away. "Look, Stevie, I admire your perseverance with this case, I really do. But your very own report here, signed by *you*" — he picked up the sheaf of papers she'd left for him first thing that morning — "tells me this case is solved.

We have enough evidence here that Gant was the killer. Now all we can do is try to find out who killed Gant, but we both know this is a piece-of-shit case."

Stevie tried to contain her exasperation. It wasn't politically smart for a rookie to challenge her superior. In fact, it was career suicide. *Oh, to hell with it! Traffic division, here I come!*

"Inspector, we could be letting someone off the hook, someone who should be in jail right now. I mean, he could kill again, for God's sake. He's already killed two people. We can't just ignore this new evidence."

McLemore's face was clenched, the veins in his neck visibly throbbing now. He wouldn't shout; it wasn't his style. But his measured voice spoke his wrath. "What other evidence? All you've got is a phone call, a phone call that was by no means even close to a confession. This isn't the Kennedy assassination, Stevie. We don't have the time or the staff to go looking for conspiracy theories around every corner. Is that understood?"

Stevie stood her stubborn ground, refusing to knuckle under. Her face was unflinching, her body straight and stiff. "All I'm asking, Inspector, is to interview Father Mark Chiarelli again. That's all."

McLemore sighed, then grimaced. "You mean that's all you're asking for today." He picked up a pencil and began angrily tapping it like a drumstick on his desktop. "All right, Stevie, just this once. But that's it. Then this case is officially closed."

She knew she shouldn't push her boss's generosity, but she couldn't help herself. "Then can I help Roulston on the Gant case?"

McLemore wanted to smile, but he wouldn't give her the satisfaction. She was one pushy broad. "All right. But that's not to say it's an excuse for you to go off chasing your conspiracy theories." He worked up his best glare. "Roulston will direct you. And if it means sweeping under his feet, that's what you'll do. Got it?"

Stevie nodded. It was as much as she could hope to get.

# CHAPTER NINE

Stevie walked up to the familiar office door at the rectory of St. Mary's and rang the bell. Her eyes grazed over the meticulously manicured lawns and immaculate flower gardens, the granite buildings frosted with ivy. The view of the city lay below like a busy quilt, stretching for miles to the south until it melted into the fine line halving the horizon and the gray-blue of Lake Ontario. The tall, needle-like CN tower was clearly visible on this crisp spring afternoon, its pulsating red clearance light faint but discernible.

The muffled city sounds could almost deceive one to thinking it was the countryside instead of a bustling city. Stevie felt the bitter irony that this place of worship and spiritual contemplation had been the scene of such violence.

"Detective Houston, isn't it?"

It was Mrs. Powers opening the door, her face prideful at having remembering Stevie's name. But her half-smile wasn't particularly welcoming.

"That's right, Mrs. Powers. May I?"

"All right. What can I do for you?"

Stevie had worn her finest threads for this occasion — charcoal wool dress trousers, the pleats honed to a sharp edge, white silk blouse, and a thick, smooth linen jacket the color of rich, red wine. Having to spend money on clothes was one of the things she disliked about being a detective.

"Actually, I'd like to talk to Father Mark Chiarelli," she said as she followed the pudgy woman and the trail of dense, cheap perfume to the reception room, the same room where she'd interviewed Mrs. Powers nine days ago after Father McCleary's body was found.

"Father just stepped out, but he should be back any time. He's a very busy man now that he has his own parish."

"You mean, he's taken over here until they assign someone else to lead the parish?"

"Oh, no, dear. This is Father Chiarelli's parish now. Auxiliary Bishop Kayson made it official last Thursday."

Stevie tried to hide the frown she felt inside. *So Father Chiarelli definitely made out all right in all of this. What a switch that would be for the congregation — a 180-degree swing from the left to the right.*

"Would you like to sit down, Detective?"

"Yes, thank you." Stevie claimed one of the seats. She noticed a fresh pot of coffee behind Mrs. Powers, but there was no forthcoming offer. The church secretary sat down behind her own small desk.

Stevie purposely left her notebook in her jacket pocket, not wanting Mrs. Powers to think this was an official police interview. It would be a perfect opportunity for a little fishing expedition. Stevie cast her line.

"I imagine Father Chiarelli is pleased with his new assignment."

Mrs. Powers smiled, clearly satisfied with her new boss, her loyalties having quickly changed. "Oh, yes, though the circumstances were simply dreadful, of course."

"Of course," Stevie repeated solemnly. "It must be quite an adjustment for the congregation."

"Everyone is still in shock with the passing of Father McCleary. But Father Chiarelli will be good for St. Mary's. For such a young man —" She checked herself, realizing that her boss was probably about the same age as Stevie. "He may not be young to you, but he is to me," she laughed artificially. "For a man his age, he has a very strong appreciation for what the Catholic Church stands for. We need more like him to lead us into the next century."

Stevie suppressed the urge to clutch her throat in a mock gagging motion. The Church needed more people like Father Gregory McCleary and Father Peter LaRoche — men who were liberal-minded enough and flexible enough to bend with the times. It wasn't easy, but she swallowed her irritation instead and played dumb. "How do you mean, Mrs. Powers?"

A condescending smile for a young woman who would simply never understand. "Detective Houston, I'm sure I don't have to tell someone in your profession that today's world is, pardon my language, going to hell in a handbasket. We need to get back to the old ways."

Stevie's eyebrows leveled. "Old ways?"

"Indeed, where God and church and family are all that matters. A return to morals and the Catholic faith."

Stevie sighed and mentally retreated from the bait. Her youthful, hotheaded side was tempted to engage her subject in a heated discussion about religion and morals, but she knew it would only get her into trouble. It wasn't worth it.

"Mrs. Powers, you said Bishop Kayson appointed Father Chiarelli as head of St. Mary's. Are they very close?"

"Oh, yes, dear. Bishop Kayson has really taken him under his wing. They have lunch together every Tuesday."

Stevie heard a door shut in another room, then the unmistakable rustling noises in what was now Father Chiarelli's office beyond a heavy mahogany door. He must have just come in through a back door.

"That must be Father now. I'll let him know you're here."

She slipped through the door, then quickly emerged.

"Father says he only has a few minutes to spare, but he'll see you now."

The young priest's drawn face betrayed his dismay at Stevie's spontaneous visit. His attempted smile, like his self-assured air, quickly fell flat. Stevie was proud of her ability to get under Father Chiarelli's skin, something he probably wasn't used to from a woman. And the fact that she was gay, well, hell, that was the icing on the cake as far as she was concerned. Stevie smiled and took a delicious chomp.

"Father Chiarelli, I'm sure you won't mind if I go through the details with you again about Father McCleary's murder."

She sat down in the leather wingback chair without being asked. After some hesitation, as if he thought that by remaining standing, this irritating cop would take the hint and leave, Chiarelli finally sat too.

He sighed, then settled back as if it were no bother at all. Stevie withdrew her notepad and made a show of slowly flipping the pages.

"You told me earlier that after you found Father McCleary, you came downstairs to this office and called Auxiliary Bishop Kayson. Is that right?"

He nodded perfunctorily.

"You told me you discussed things like protocol — how to handle the congregation, the media, etcetera. Is that correct?"

Another trite nod.

"Did the topic of the police come up?"

"No, Detective Houston. We had no reason to believe it was a murder."

"I see. And did you tell the Bishop exactly what you'd seen upstairs?"

Chiarelli cleared his throat and swallowed hard. *Don't tell me you actually feel badly,* Stevie thought bitterly.

"No, I didn't. I was upset, shocked at what I'd seen. I just said Father McCleary was dead, that I'd seen him myself."

Stevie paused, pretending to study her notes. "When I interviewed you last, you said that after you spoke with Bishop Kayson, you went upstairs for a second time to check for a pulse, to make sure Father McCleary was actually dead." She looked up, her dark brown eyes like quicksand. "You just said you told Bishop Kayson that Father McCleary was clearly dead. So why *did* you go up that second time?"

Another swallow, but the face remained clenched, fallow. "After I told Bishop Kayson he was dead, I thought I'd better really make sure. One wouldn't want to be wrong about that sort of thing."

"And did the Bishop ask you how he'd died?"

A twist of discomfort in Chiarelli, as if it just occurred to him that perhaps the Bishop should have asked him the details. It was barely discernible, but Stevie picked up on his quickened breathing, the twitch in his left eye. "No, he did not ask."

Stevie's eyes poked at the priest, drilling into him her unspoken impatience. "But it was hardly the way you would expect to find someone, tied up at the neck and wearing women's underwear."

"I, I didn't want to upset the Bishop. It, the whole thing was rather embarrassing."

A new test for him: "Father, someone phoned the newspaper the other night, someone all too happy to talk about how Father McCleary died, about his 'little problem.' You wouldn't know anything about that, would you?"

Chiarelli narrowed his eyes, his voice rising. "Of course not! I don't believe in airing the Church's" — he cast his eyes about — "dirty laundry in public."

Now she was ready to really make him squirm. "Father Chiarelli, what do you know about a man by the name of Jonathon Gant?"

Stevie got her wish. A film of sweat began lining his forehead, and the ice in his blue eyes began to splinter.

He hesitated, started to say something, then closed his mouth again to try to compose himself first. He sucked in a chest full of air. "I believe I have heard the name somewhere. I'm just not sure in what capacity."

"Then let me refresh your memory, Father. Jonathon Gant and Father McCleary had a relationship about twenty years ago in North Bay. Gant was just a teenager at the time, and when the affair became known, Father McCleary was shipped south."

Chiarelli exhaled and nodded resignedly. "Yes, that's where I've heard the name." He shook his head in scorn. "I'm afraid Father McCleary's career was tainted from the very beginning."

"That's not what I heard," Stevie disagreed, jabbing the needle in farther. "I heard Father McCleary was getting along quite well in the arch-diocese, and that the archbishop was considering promoting him to one of the auxiliary bishop positions, possibly at the expense of your friend, Bishop Kayson," she gambled.

A red tide roared up the priest's neck and settled in his face, neck veins throbbing in anger. "That would never have happened," came the choked reply through clenched teeth.

Stevie's smile was cocky, her tone mocking. "You might never have gotten your own parish if Father McCleary had moved up, no? After all, your views were quite opposite."

Chiarelli was shaking with fury. Unknowingly he was wringing his hands, the silver of his Medic Alert bracelet glinting in the afternoon light that streamed through the window. He had blown his cool, and it was too late to get it back. This bitch had played him like a fiddle.

"Look, Detective, if you're suggesting I had anything to do with Father McCleary's untimely death, I'll have a slander suit on you so fast you'll be back pounding the pavement before you ever know what hit you."

Stevie huffed her disbelief.

"I have nothing more to say. If you have any more questions of me, you'll have to talk to my lawyer!"

Stevie stood, squaring her broad shoulders victoriously, her hand purposely sweeping over the corner of his desk and knocking a pen set to the floor.

"Sorry about that," she smiled as she watched him reach with his left hand to retrieve it. "I don't have any more questions, Father, you've answered them all perfectly. By the way," she cast over her shoulder, "did you know that Jonathon Gant was found murdered on the weekend?"

As she opened the door to leave, Stevie turned to watch the reaction. The bruising anger had quickly drained from Chiarelli, his face as blanched as a freshly peeled apple, eyes pinched in shock. She hoped that whatever that Medic Alert bracelet on him was for, it wasn't a heart condition. Stevie left him that way — alone, shocked, and fearful. A cool draft followed her outside.

Stevie relaxed into Jade's busy fingers, her neck and shoulders melting beneath her touch. The massage, combined with the glass of red wine in her fist, was just the tonic she needed after that interview with Chiarelli. That and the mountain of computer printouts and reports she found piled on her desktop when she'd returned to the office.

Roulston had left the two-foot-high pile for her — reports of every stolen .22 caliber rifle and handgun in Metropolitan Toronto from the last ten years. Preliminary examination of the bullet had proved of little help yet. It would be weeks before the Center of Forensic Sciences, just a few blocks from police headquarters, would be able to narrow the weapon down to a particular make and size.

Stevie had worked well into the evening sorting the reports into handguns versus rifles. Jade was fairly certain a handgun had been used because of the telltale tattooing on Gant's head that indicated that the barrel had fired just inches from the entry wound. That and the fact that it would be next to impossible to wander around downtown with a rifle and not be noticed. So she'd start with those first, but it would still take days to get through them all, she complained to Jade.

Keeping Stevie buried in paperwork was

Roulston's way of getting her out of his hair, *the prick!* The stolen gun reports would be a tremendous long shot, Stevie knew. Guns were difficult to buy legally in Canada. Hell, even to buy ammunition in the province of Ontario you had to show ID and sign for it. Most of the weapons used in criminal activities had been stolen and sold on the black market. But if the original owner of the gun that killed Gant could be found, just maybe, through other items stolen in a break-in for example, they could trace the gun's path to the killer.

Jade pulled the glass from Stevie's hand and set it on the coffee table in front of them. Nuzzling into Stevie's neck, she planted soft, wet kisses on her lover then whispered in her ear. "Enough about this case for one night. I've got plans for you!"

Abruptly, Stevie squeezed out of her grasp, scooped up her wineglass, and sauntered over to the large window, distracted eyes resting on the darkened lake below, but not really seeing.

Jade sighed. *Now what?* Was Stevie getting squeamish again about getting too close? In frustration, she buried her face in her hands and gently rubbed her forehead. Every time Stevie pulled away from her, would she forever have to wonder what she'd done to make her feel smothered, or whatever the hell it was she was feeling? *It would be so damn easy to give up on her,* Jade thought. Just walk away from her and all her relationship phobias! Another sigh. Who the hell was she kidding? She was hooked on this cop, this woman whose uniform of armor extended to her heart.

But Jade knew there was goodness, gentleness and, yes, vulnerability hidden deep inside, there for her to mine. She went to Stevie and hugged her from behind. "I'm sorry."

Stevie turned around, bewilderment flashing in her eyes. "Sorry for what?"

Jade shrugged. "For whatever I said that made you withdraw from me."

Another puzzled look, as if someone had just splashed her with cold water. "What are you talking about, Jade?"

"I'm talking about what just happened, about you withdrawing from me as soon as I started getting romantic."

"I did?"

Jade's irritation turned to just plain pissed off. "Hello? You don't have the slightest idea of what I'm talking about, do you?"

Stevie's forehead furrowed. "Look, you're trying to pick a fight with me, and I haven't even done anything!"

Jade bit her tongue, the temptation to slap her lover silly just a pulse away. "Stephanie Houston, you're the most frustrating woman I've ever known! It was like I wasn't even here. You just shut me out like you were closing a door and going into another room or something."

Stevie's head tersely shook in disagreement. "I was just thinking about the case, that's all. I swear. I don't know why you're making such a big deal over it."

"Because when you went off in that world of yours, it was like you were rejecting me, like you were having second thoughts about us."

Stevie's eyes widened. *Christ, so that's what this is all about. Talk about sensitive.* She couldn't even take a few minutes out to think without Jade looking for something to be wrong. She would have rolled her eyes if Jade hadn't been right there, full moist eyes reading Stevie's face. *Jesus, she even looks like she's going to cry.*

Stevie pulled Jade into her and held her tightly, pressing into her small but firm body. The smell of Jade's hair, her flesh, even her soap, filled Stevie's ravenous lungs, intoxicating her until she felt their bodies begin to sway slightly.

*All right, Jade's right.* She was being an ass just switching off like that. And Jade had every right to be on tenterhooks about their relationship after all the avoidance games Stevie had played.

"I'm sorry, Jade, you were right about me withdrawing." She pulled back, her hand moving to Jade's chin. "But I wasn't withdrawing from you. At least, I wasn't trying to. I was withdrawing into my case, that's all it was."

Those hypnotic green eyes were still moist, still at the bursting point, and at that very moment Stevie's heart brimmed with love.

"Just don't shut me out, Stevie, about anything. You can talk to me about your case or anything that's bothering you. I thought you knew that."

"I do know that, Jade. I just forget sometimes that there's another half of me now."

Jade smiled, her eyes ablaze. "You really mean that, the half thing?"

"Of course! I love you, Jade. I love you like" — her eyes cast around wildly as her mind raced mischievously — "like a triple-dip chocolate ice-cream cone with sprinkles on top!"

Jade laughed so hard she thought she'd crumple.

"I love you like an ice cold beer on a hot summer day, like, like an exit ramp on the Gardiner Expressway at rush hour!"

Another peel of gut-wrenching laughter.

"Like double wool socks on an Arctic hike, like —"

"All right, all right," Jade yelped. "You love me, you love me!"

Stevie reached down to the firm curve of Jade's ass and hoisted her up until Jade was looking down at her. The thirty- or forty-pound weight difference between them allowed for such romantic frolic.

"God, I love you!" Jade burst out.

Stevie spun her around and around until Jade begged her to stop, then kissed her fully.

Their lovemaking was just as exuberant, consuming every sweaty fiber of them both in a raucous, exhaustive, horizontal dance. Stevie felt her razor-sharp emotions and raw passion drain from her body as Jade brought her to orgasm. Silently, as they clutched one another in the darkness, Stevie wondered if their physical intensity had somehow been honed to a fine edge by all the ugliness they'd both seen in their lives — Jade in the morgue, and Stevie on the streets. It was as if they both realized how precious any beauty and goodness was, and how fleeting it could be. She kissed Jade's forehead.

Jade grinned back. "What were you mulling over about your case earlier?"

"You mean before our fight?" Stevie smiled. "Our first fight!"

"You have to admit it was fun making up!"

Stevie giggled. "I can see how a fight a week could be good for a relationship."

"Forget it. Let's just pretend to fight and make up anyway."

"Agreed." Stevie's smile dimmed as her mind tunneled into the McCleary case again. "I was thinking about my interview with Chiarelli. He's definitely nervous about something."

"You think he's the one behind all this?"

Stevie shook her head. "I can't see him getting his hands dirty murdering people. He was shocked when I told him about Gant's murder, and he doesn't shock easily. He even looked scared, Jade. Damn scared."

"Scared of what, do you suppose?"

"I don't know. Like he wasn't expecting this. Like maybe he's into something way over his head."

"Hmmm. Well, if he knows something, maybe he'll crack."

"He definitely knows more than he's telling me. I've got to go see this Kayson, the auxiliary bishop. They seem to be good buddies, and Kayson too had something to gain with McCleary's death. Kayson was the first person Chiarelli called when he found McCleary dead."

"I thought your inspector told you your interview with Chiarelli was your last hurrah."

Stevie shrugged. "I can't stop now, Jade. I'm on to something, I can feel it."

"Yeah, well, feel this, baby." Jade rolled on top of her, her fingers finding all of Stevie's buttons. She lit them up like a Christmas tree, one bulb at a time.

# CHAPTER TEN

Bishop Anton Kayson's office was as opulent as Stevie had imagined. The mahogany desk was large and imposing, its ornateness further reminding visitors of their smallness, their insignificance. Expensive paintings in thick gilded frames hung on the walls, all perfectly straight. A large walled bookshelf was filled with leather-bound books, and on the table behind the desk stood an autographed, framed photo of Kayson with the pope.

At Kayson's invitation, Stevie sat on the velvet chair opposite his desk. He hadn't seemed surprised or dismayed at her unannounced visit this Tuesday morning. In fact his face had registered nothing much at all when she'd showed up, his calmness hinting that'd he'd almost been expecting her one of these days. He was a cool customer, much tougher than Chiarelli. What had she expected? A marshmallow?

Kayson's appearance was that of a simple working man, approachable and down to earth in his black slacks, short-sleeved black shirt, and clerical collar. But Stevie knew better than to underestimate this politically astute man. The size and decor of his office, his flawlessly polished shoes, the thick gemmed rings on his fingers, the pearl-and-gold cross pendant around his neck, the Rolex watch, his carefully barbered, graying hair, the faint scent of expensive cologne all told Stevie this was a man who paid great attention to detail and image.

As she explained her presence, Kayson, a tall and still stocky man in his late fifties, listened while reaching into a desk drawer with his left hand. He pulled out an exquisitely carved pipe — a meerschaum, Stevie recognized. From the same drawer he pinched a wad of tobacco from a pouch and patiently tamped it into the bowl, lighting it with a gold lighter — twenty-four karat, Stevie guessed. The rich aroma filled the room with a thin fog, reminding Stevie of her father.

"How can I help you, Officer?" he finally asked, a superficial smile on his face. "I'm afraid I really don't know much about Father McCleary's death, though I certainly wish there was something I could do to help you find whoever is responsible."

Stevie uttered her appreciation, then launched into her questions. "Why do you think you were the first

**119**

person Father Chiarelli called after he found Father McCleary?"

Kayson's eyes moved slightly before resting on Stevie. "You would have to ask him for certain. But as the superior of both men, certainly I would want to know as quickly as possible. I would not have wanted to hear about it on the radio that evening or from a police officer, a stranger. Surely you can understand that."

His tone was even and authoritative, as though his were the only opinions or logical answers. He possessed a quiet but all-encompassing arrogance, probably from decades of acting as God's personal emissary. Stevie was glad she hadn't been raised Catholic and wasn't hypnotized by the spell of religion. Still, Catholicism and its trappings was intimidating.

"If you can remember back to that phone call, Bishop, what do you recall of it?"

Another quiet pull on the pipe, another cloud of tobacco smoke. The man had no intention of acting bothered by Stevie's visit, even though his weekly lunch with Chiarelli was approaching. *This week they'll certainly have something to talk about.* Stevie smiled to herself.

"He was rather upset when he told me Father McCleary was dead, that he'd seen him for himself. I tried to calm him, asked him if he was sure."

"And was he?"

"Yes," Kayson answered gravely.

"And what else did you discuss?"

Kayson sat very still, his brown eyes a mask, the only movement coming from his left hand containing the pipe. "I told him that for the time being it would

120

be wise not to discuss anything with anyone but the police. I told him that we would meet later to discuss funeral details and the operation of St. Mary's. I then urged him to get himself together, that others would be counting on him."

"And that's it?"

The Bishop simply smiled his agreement.

Stevie was eager for the next segment of the interview, though she knew any gains would be small.

"I trust you know the circumstances of Father McCleary's death, Bishop Kayson?"

He nodded, thin lips slightly pursed. "Very unfortunate. A very sad and degrading way to end such a profitable life."

His last words ignited Stevie's attention. "Father McCleary's career wasn't always stellar, I understand."

If she was expecting a denial, she didn't get it.

"That's true. He had a rough time earlier on, but the Church dealt with it and he was able to put it behind him."

Stevie took a deep breath and plunged in. "Are you saying the Church looked the other way when it came to Father McCleary's homosexuality?"

There was no hesitation, as if the bishop had long ago planned his answer. "We do not cast people aside for such a flaw." Stevie frowned at the word *flaw*. Oblivious to her response, he continued expansively, as if performing. "Father McCleary had much to offer to this archdiocese and to his congregation, and indeed to the community at large. What he did for people with AIDS and others of that persuasion was honorable. As for his personal life, Detective Houston, we believed he could have been helped."

Stevie's eyebrows gave away her surprise at Kayson's seeming understanding. "So you didn't have a problem with his ideals? I mean, he seemed to be a real moderate."

"I had no problem with Father McCleary's ideals. In fact, I was supportive of him. You see, Detective, we need moderates in our Church to keep a workable balance."

Stevie's eyes narrowed, disbelieving. "You mean to balance more conservative ideals such as your own." She wasn't going to let him think she was just some dumb cop.

His smile was condescending. "Why, it's no secret my ideals differed from Father McCleary's. But that doesn't mean we can't be understanding of views that vary from our own. After all, we in the Church all have the same goals, the same loyalties."

"So it was okay with you that Father McCleary was politically gaining ground within the archdiocese. That the archbishop was more than willing to listen to his moderate ideals." She fired away at him like a machine gun. "It was okay with you that you were on the way down and Father McCleary was on the way up. That your views were quickly becoming outdated and nonprogressive in a faith struggling to keep its congregations and to attract young people."

The silence that followed was palpable. Kayson simply stared at Stevie with eyes so cool and calculating it was almost frightening. When he finally spoke, it was in his usual dry tone, his voice as crisp as a cold winter day.

"Young lady, I don't know where you got your information but I can assure you that you have greatly exaggerated. I have never had any reason to believe that I was on the way down as you so mistakenly put it. Nor was there any movement afoot to give Father McCleary an increased role in the archdiocese. The work he was doing at the ground level was very important." Another pitying smile.

"Obviously, you do not know much about the Catholic faith. Catholicism is a compassionate religion, and it has not survived for centuries without good reason. There is always room in our religion for people like myself as well as Father McCleary."

Kayson set his pipe down and stood. "If there is nothing further, I have work to do."

He did not shake Stevie's hand or offer any verbal pleasantries as she left. She smiled. She had gotten under his skin after all.

Stevie took the stairs to the third floor at police headquarters and was quickly intercepted by Judy, the homicide squad receptionist.

"Hey Stevie, this came for you." She handed Stevie a large, plain manilla envelope.

"Thanks," Stevie said, turning it over in her hands. It was simply marked, in large printed letters, DETECTIVE S. HOUSTON, METRO TORONTO POLICE, HOMICIDE DEPT.

"Did somebody drop it off?" she asked the secretary.

"It was left at the main desk downstairs this morning. Oh, and Inspector McLemore said to tell you he wants to see you the minute you get in."

Stevie rolled her eyes and hurried to her desk. Shoving the piles of stolen gun reports aside, she sat down and tore the envelope open. There was no note or letter indicating where it had come from or what it was about; just a two-page photocopy of a typed report on Toronto Archdiocese letterhead.

Stevie quickly scanned the report, which was dated just two months ago. The word CONFIDENTIAL was boldly typed across the top, and it was addressed to the archbishop himself. The report, from a committee within the archdiocese, recommended more tolerance for the poor, for broken homes, for different ethnic groups, and — there it was — homosexuals as a way of bolstering thinning congregations. Father Gregory McCleary and St. Mary's Church were singled out further on as prime examples of how the archdiocese could still thrive in a large, modern city such as Toronto. The last paragraph was a recommendation that Father McCleary be given a more prominent and visible role in the archdiocese, and that certain unnamed, very visible but regressive leaders be relegated to less prominent roles.

Stevie smiled at the confirmation of her suspicions. If she was reading this report, surely Bishop Kayson had seen it as well, *the lying bastard.*

She didn't recognize any of the names of the committee members, nor was there any indication of their ranks within the archdiocese. Stevie had already done her homework. She knew the archdiocese was the largest in Canada, with four auxiliary bishops, more than three hundred priests, and even more nuns. Then there were the laymen and civilian staff — people like Mrs. Powers. There would be no way to know who had leaked the report to Stevie, though Father Peter LaRoche would be a likely candidate. But still, if it had been him, why had he not simply asked to meet her and given it to her in person? He had already told her much of what the report contained.

Stevie slipped the report back in the envelope. Maybe it was Chiarelli. When she had left him yesterday, he'd looked pale as a ghost, the tarnish of a man burdened with fear. Perhaps he was afraid he was next, and in his own backward way, had decided to talk. She'd go see him later today, that's what she'd do. And if she couldn't make him talk, she'd feel him out, see if there was some hint that he was behind this.

"Houston!"

The sudden presence of her inspector startled Stevie. The look on his face was even more unsettling.

"You were supposed to report to me as soon as you got in." He didn't wait for an excuse. He jerked his head in the direction of his office. "Now."

Stevie grabbed the envelope and followed him to his office, where he closed the door behind her with an ominous thud.

"What the hell were you doing at Bishop Kayson's this morning?"

"Interviewing him, sir. I thought he might have some information that would be helpful. And besides, I wanted to confirm the phone call Chiarelli said he'd made to him after he found the body."

McLemore continued standing behind his desk, a bad sign. Stevie stood too. There would be nothing chummy about this little chat. She knew she was in the doghouse, big time.

"I thought I told you no more hotdogging around with this case. Was I not clear enough?"

Stevie swallowed her insolence. "Yes, sir, you were."

"Kayson's none too happy with your visit. He was pretty hot about it, actually. He called Superintendent Greene to complain, and now Greene's riding my ass about you."

Stevie bit the inside of her cheek, then decided to take her best shot, waving the envelope in front of her. "Someone anonymously dropped this report off to me today. It's from a committee within the archdiocese, recommending McCleary be promoted. It confirms everything I'd been told."

McLemore took the envelope from her and silently scanned the report, his forehead still wrinkled in skepticism, his eyes unblinking. "This still doesn't point the way to Kayson or Chiarelli, if that's what you're driving at with this."

"But Kayson lied to me this morning. He told me there was no such movement within the archdiocese to promote McCleary, when obviously there was, and it was likely going to be at his expense."

McLemore shook his head vehemently. "Look, it's just some confidential report that Kayson probably didn't even know about."

"Ha," Stevie retorted, her humility out the window. "You can bet there isn't a thing that goes on in that archdiocese that Kayson doesn't know about. He smells, Inspector."

McLemore began pacing, his body stiff. "Stevie, you've got zilch on Kayson or Chiarelli. There's not even remotely reasonable and probable grounds enough to do anything with either of them." He stopped in front of her. "We have the evidence that

Gant killed McCleary, in case you've forgotten. That means this case is closed. Got it?"

After some hesitation, which only further riled her boss, Stevie nodded.

"Look Stevie, this isn't some hit TV show. We work as a team here, and if you can't be a team player, then traffic is a good place for people who like to work alone."

He let his veiled threat wash over Stevie until he noticed the tiny slump melt her shoulders and the rebellious spark in her eyes die out.

"Don't make yourself a liability around here. Now, don't you have some stolen gun reports to get back to?"

"Yes, sir."

Stevie spent the rest of the afternoon poring over the reports, finally making a dent in them, but there were still a couple of dozen to go.

To hell with it, she finally shrugged, as the early evening sunlight bathed the office in a dusky light. It was too nice an evening after too long a day to spend another minute inside.

Stevie gathered her jacket from the coatrack near her desk, locked her gun away in her locker, and headed out to the underground garage where her dark green Mustang convertible was parked. The push of a button sent the top down as Stevie pulled out into the downtown dinner-hour traffic, the fading May sun still warm and refreshing. June was just around the corner, and she could hardly wait for T-shirts and shorts weather. Maybe she and Jade could get out of town one of these weekends, maybe rent a cottage up north around Georgian Bay. The thought of the two of them skinny-dipping under a midnight moon set off a smile on Stevie's face and a whole set of new fantasies in her head.

But her mind quickly wandered. Instead of heading to her Cabbagetown digs, or Jade's harborside apartment, Stevie found herself driving north on Yonge toward St. Mary's.

She just had to talk to Chiarelli again, to see if he was finally ready to spill whatever he knew, to ask him if he'd sent her that report.

Heading up the winding drive of the church, it once again reminded her of the original sudden death call they'd gotten a week and a half ago. A lot of people's lives had changed since then — hers, Jade's, Jovanowski's, Chiarelli's, even Mrs. Powers.

Stevie was surprised to see a marked police cruiser as she pulled into the parking area. So far as she knew, the case was closed. So what the hell were uniforms doing here?

Stevie took her badge out for the young woman officer outside the parish office. "What's going on here?"

"Sudden death, Detective Houston. About an hour ago. We were just leaving. I didn't know homicide was called on this."

"We weren't," Stevie said. "I was just in the neighborhood. What's happened?"

"Young priest, name of Chiarelli, found dead in the rectory by the church secretary."

"Aw, Christ!" Stevie swore. "What happened to him?"

"Coroner's already come and gone. Body's gone too. Looks like natural causes, no signs of anything unusual."

Stevie's heart felt like it was rolling downhill, sweat trickling down her sides. *Shit,* she should have seen this coming. The guy was practically shaking with fear yesterday. *Natural causes, my ass!*

"We should have been called to this. Where's your sergeant?"

The young woman, probably still a rookie, Stevie guessed, grew defensive. "He just left. Look, it didn't fit the criteria for calling in homicide. There weren't any signs of foul play or unnatural trauma. The guy just collapsed."

"There was a murder right here a week and a half ago, for crissakes. Where's Mrs. Powers?"

"She was pretty upset. We sent her home with her husband."

Stevie stalked back to her car. Where the hell was Jovanowski when she needed him?

# CHAPTER ELEVEN

Stevie worked herself into a sweat on the drive back to headquarters. If she'd had a mouth full of nails, she'd have spit every one at her inspector. If only McLemore had taken her more seriously and not constantly thrown roadblocks in her path, maybe Chiarelli would still be alive. Or maybe if she'd told McLemore to go screw himself ... Hell, Stevie breathed. If she'd done that, she'd be back in uniform right now.

Her gut told her it was Chiarelli who had anonymously given her that archdiocese report this morning, and somehow, someone — Kayson maybe? — had found out and quickly taken action. Like dominoes, nearly everyone connected to this case, anyone who might know something, was turning up dead. Every potential leak was being plugged. So where did that leave her? With a big fat, fucking zero.

Upon reaching headquarters, Stevie immediately phoned the commanding officer of the division responsible for the investigation. And just as she'd been told at the scene, there was no foul play suspected. Further investigation was stalled until they could get an autopsy report back. She demanded, much to the sergeant's chagrin, that the officer's preliminary report be faxed to her as soon as possible.

Killing time, Stevie punched the buttons on her desk phone, hoisting her tired legs onto her desk.

"Hi sweetie, it's me."

"Stevie, where are you?"

Stevie moaned her exhaustion. "Sorry, I'm still at work. You'll never guess what's happened."

"What?" Jade asked worriedly. "Are you okay?"

"I'm fine, but Father Chiarelli's definitely not. He's dead."

"What do you mean? What happened?"

Stevie briefly explained the day's events, including her visit earlier with Kayson.

"C'mon over and we'll talk about it," Jade urged.

"I can't. I need to hang around here for a fax. But believe me, I'd love to be over there right now. I'm barely hanging onto this case by a thread. I don't want to give up now."

Jade choked down her frustration. Loving a cop

131

was going to take a lot of patience. Loving with Stevie was going to take even more. "Can I help?"

"Actually, yes." Stevie pulled her legs down, urgency in her voice. "They were taking Chiarelli to St. Michael's Hospital for an autopsy. You know anybody over there?"

"Sure. Do you want me to see what I can find out?"

"Please. That'd be great, honey. It'll save me a few hours and a hell of a lot of red tape if you can get me the cause of death ASAP."

"You got it. But I want you to know something. If you weren't so cute, you'd be out of luck. Hey, you must be planning on being done sometime tonight. Why don't you come over? I'll wait up."

Stevie's smile dissolved. "I'd love to, but I don't know how long I'll be. And by then, I wouldn't be good for anything anyway."

Jade let a few seconds of silence convey her disappointment. "All right. I miss you though. And I'll call you as soon as I know anything."

Stevie forced herself to wade back into the stolen gun reports between dashes to the fax machine, which was conveniently located next to the pop machine. For what her throbbing head told her was about the hundredth time, she retrieved a can of Coke and gulped it down.

Maybe she'd eat better now that she was about to settle down into married life, she consoled herself back at her desk, the pile of reports beckoning out the corner of her eye. "Shit," she cursed out loud, self-pity weighing in her belly. It was almost midnight now and here she was, sifting through a pile of reports that would get her nowhere while her case was spinning out of control. Not only that, but the hottest woman she'd ever known — her woman — was home in bed right now. Alone. *Isn't that just the icing on the goddamned cake.*

When the fax finally came, Stevie's reddened eyes brightened when she read, not surprisingly, that Auxiliary Bishop Anton Kayson was the last person believed to have seen Father Chiarelli alive. He'd brought take-out lunch to Chiarelli's private quarters at the rectory of St. Mary's, where they'd eaten. A telephone call to Kayson by the investigating officers had revealed little: The bishop had noticed nothing out of the ordinary about Father Chiarelli, and all was fine when he'd left.

Stevie slowly shook her head. She'd just see about that. Her instincts were coming to life. Kayson was getting smellier all the time.

The ring of the telephone invaded Stevie's slumber, first melding into her dream, then finally dragging her kicking and screaming into semi-alertness.

With one eye, she glanced at her bedside clock. *Christ!* 8:30 A.M. She should be clawing her way to work by now with all the other downtown traffic, not just getting out of bed! McLemore would have her for breakfast over this one.

Stevie frantically pawed at her night table until she blindly found the telephone receiver.

"Yeah!" she barked into it.

"Geez, Stevie, I hope you're not like this every morning, or I might have to leave you at the altar." It was Jade, feigning seriousness.

Stevie laughed. "Sorry, dear. I slept in."

"Late night, eh?"

"Yeah," Stevie groaned, sitting up and swinging her naked legs over the side of the bed. "And for more fun, I'm going to have to pay Kayson another visit this morning, since he was the last one to see Chiarelli alive."

"You might want to visit St. Mary's first."

"Why, what's up?"

"They just finished the postmortem on Chiarelli. Looks like he died from a bee sting."

"What?" Stevie asked, incredulous.

"He had an allergy, even had a Medic Alert bracelet warning of it. He went into anaphylactic shock almost immediately."

"What's that mean?"

"Means his bronchial tubes seized up and, essentially, he suffocated. What he needed when he started seizing up was a shot of epinephrine to counteract it. Most people who are aware they have fatal allergies have their own kits pretty close by at all times, at least I sure as hell would."

Stevie anxiously raked her fingers through her tousled hair. "You're right. I better get over there and find out where that kit was and why the hell he didn't use it. Look, I'll call you later, hon, and I owe you."

"Damn right you do. I'm holding you to me — it, I mean."

\* \* \* \* \*

134

Stevie drove directly to the church, using her cellular phone to leave a cryptic message with the office. The less McLemore knew right now, the more time she could buy.

After Stevie informed Mrs. Powers what had caused Father Chiarelli's death, the woman had raised her quivering hand to her mouth, her eyes wide in disbelief.

"Did you know he was allergic to bee stings?"

"Yes, he, he even had a Medic Alert bracelet. Oh, my, I just can't believe this has happened again."

Large tears spilled down her fleshy cheeks, her whole body quaking in a giant sob.

Stevie ushered the woman to a chair and squatted in front of her. "I know you've been through a lot, Mrs. Powers. But I need your help. Can you do that?"

Like a child being reprimanded, the woman nodded and sniffed back her tears.

"Did Father Chiarelli tell you what to do to help him if he got stung by a bee?"

Another nod. "He told me I would have to give him a needle."

Stevie breathed a sigh of relief. "And did he tell you where he kept that needle?"

"Yes. He said there was one in the bottom left drawer of his desk, and just after he moved into the rectory, he told me there was one in the silverware drawer of the kitchen."

Another pang of relief. "All right, good. You're doing fine, Mrs. Powers. What we need to do now is see if those kits are still where they're supposed to be."

They checked the office first and found the plastic

kit with all its contents intact — the small vial still sealed. Next they climbed the familiar staircase to the apartment.

The kitchen was tidy but for the sink full of dishes, probably left over from lunch with Kayson. Her eyes zeroed in on an open drawer and instinctively she knew it must be the silverware drawer. Stevie rushed to it, first peering inside, then urgently rooting around. Nothing but utensils. No needle, no vial of medicine.

"Maybe he'd moved it and just forgot to tell you," Stevie suggested calmly, not wanting to alarm the woman.

Hastily, they searched other drawers and shelves in the apartment, but there was no sign of the other kit. A dull buzzing halted Stevie at the bedroom window. Pulling the blinds aside, she spotted the diminutive culprits — three live bumblebees and two dead ones curled up on the sill.

"It has to be here somewhere," Mrs. Powers gestured with outstretched arms, oblivious to Stevie's find. "He was very careful about his health. He told me once that if he ever got stung, he only had a couple of minutes to get that needle in him. I can't believe he would have let such an important thing slip. It's just so awful."

Again she melted into sobs, leaning heavily against an open door frame for support.

Stevie waited a moment, trying to summon some sympathy for her, some feeling, but finding only hollow manners. "Mrs. Powers, I know this is difficult, but I still need your help. I need for you to keep checking around to see if you can find that kit in here, okay?"

Stevie knew it would be all right for the woman to rummage around, because this was never going to be given over to her department to investigate. It wouldn't be a crime scene, not officially, because there was no evidence a crime had been committed. That's why a hospital pathologist, and not a forensic pathologist like Jade, conducted the autopsy.

Frustration lapped at Stevie like the waves of a churning sea. *If this isn't a crime scene, then I'm Mother Teresa.*

She took Mrs. Powers by the elbow and helped her down the stairs. "Have you noticed a lot of bumblebees around here lately, Mrs. Powers?"

The woman thought for a moment. "No, I don't think so. In fact, I'm sure. Because of Father Chiarelli's problem, I would have noticed. And so would he."

Odd, Stevie concluded. It wasn't even June yet. She was no naturalist or bee expert, but she knew the pesky things didn't usually reach their peak until midsummer, when the weather was hot and humid. In fact, she hadn't even noticed one yet this year — until today.

# CHAPTER TWELVE

"But Chiarelli's dead, Inspector!"

"I know Stevie, you said that twice already in the last two minutes." McLemore was his usual gruff self, at least, usual these days in dealing with Stevie.

No matter how many lectures, it just wasn't sinking into her thick skull. She was a freshman, a rookie, a detective constable, not the Bionic Woman! She was already pissing off everybody else in the squad with her hotdogging, and even Superintendent Greene had noticed how she was quickly getting beyond control. Meaning that if he, McLemore, didn't soon tether her, his own ass would be on the line.

Stevie plowed on. "Don't you find it the least bit odd that this man died of a fatal bee sting so close on the heels of McCleary, just when he was starting to crack? And where did that epinephrine kit go? And bees in May —"

"Stevie, enough!" he cut her off. "We've already skated on this rink. Yes, it's all a strange coincidence. But that's life, for God's sake!"

"I know Inspector, but come on!" Stevie's own temper ignited.

"No, you come on!" her superior shouted, his voice carrying beyond the closed door, as the startled glances outside his office confirmed.

McLemore leapt up and closed the blinds of the window looking out into the squad room, his hand quivering with anger. When he settled back in his chair, he steepled his hands on his desk and closed his eyes momentarily, drawing on whatever composure he could invoke.

"Stevie, I shouldn't have to explain the rules of evidence to you. There is no evidence of a crime here. And as for the McCleary case —"

"But Inspector," she rudely interrupted, "we've got to keep the case open, that's all I'm asking."

The smoldering in his eyes exploded into a raging blaze, a rarity for him. "Detective Houston, I've had enough of your insubordination and your wild speculation!" He stood, hands tightly clasping the edge of his desk, his jaw clenched. "You have chosen to ignore all the warning signs I've given you. You are still on probation with this squad, and yet you act like you have all the answers. You don't need anyone, do you?"

Stevie was silent, returning his stony gaze with a look of quiet defiance.

McLemore nodded unhappily. "That's what I thought. Stevie Houston, the Lone Ranger. Let me tell you something. We don't operate that way here. We work together, as a team, gathering evidence one piece at a time in a methodical manner until there is enough to make an arrest and get a conviction. We don't storm in, guns blazing, and round everyone up and haul 'em off to jail like the wild west or something. Do you understand?"

Stevie exhaled testily. "Yes, sir."

McLemore paused, then paced behind his desk, his head bent in serious consideration. When he stopped in front of Stevie, she took the cue and stood also.

"This is your final warning, Stevie. From now until my say-so, you will stick with Detective Roulston like gum to a running shoe. You will report directly to him, and I want him knowing every hour, every minute, where you're at and what you're up to. Is that clear?"

"Yes, sir."

"I cannot stress enough to you how serious I am about this, Stevie." The anger had drained from McLemore's face, now limp with either weariness or disappointment, Stevie wasn't sure which. "I think you could have what it takes to be a very good detective, it's why you're here. But I'm watching you like a hawk. Any more nonsense, and you're out. I'll personally see that you're knocked back to patrol."

\* \* \* \* \*

Stevie's body slumped in one giant sigh in her chair, her eyes glazed and unfocused. Her anger and self-righteousness had yielded to injured pride. She was so sure she was right about Kayson being behind all the killings. At least Jade believed in her, and maybe Jovanowski.

She sat that way for about an hour until she finally gave herself a mental kick in the butt, resigning herself to finishing what was left of the stolen gun reports on her desk. She rolled up her sleeves and unfastened her pistol and shoulder holster, draping the cumbersome pile of leather and metal over the back of her chair. It would be one long afternoon after one hell of a morning. She hoped Jade would be home with a nice bottle of wine, or a bottle of *something,* by the time she finished.

By late afternoon, Stevie's back had begun to ache, and her eyes stung from weariness. She pulled another report from the pile and flipped it open.

It took a few seconds for her mind to process what her eyes saw. Then, as though the report itself were on fire, she dropped it on her desk. The information it contained ignited every nerve in her body. Her heart nearly stopped; she had to remind herself to breathe.

Anton Kayson had reported that his .22 semi-automatic handgun had been stolen from the glove box of his car after he'd stopped at a corner store on his way to target practice. The bishop was a member of a gun club, his hobby was target shooting, and he possessed all the legal documents for owning and carrying a gun, so long as he was carrying the gun to a bona fide target range. The report, Stevie read

141

in astonishment, was filed with police just three weeks ago.

"Hey, Roulston," she yelled breathlessly across the squad room as she hurried to his desk. "Take a look at this!" She tossed the report on his desk, smiling triumphantly.

He scanned it quickly, his face sour when he looked up. "Yeah, so?"

"So Kayson reported his gun — a .22 — stolen just three weeks ago! I'd bet you my car it was the same gun used on Gant."

Roulston harrumphed. "What gives you that idea?"

"Look, if you were planning on using a gun in a criminal act, wouldn't you report it stolen first? Then if it's ever traced back to you, you could just point to the stolen gun report and claim some punk must have used it."

Roulston frowned. "That's really stretching it, Houston. Geez, you've really got a hard-on for nailing this Kayson, don't you?"

Stevie rolled her eyes. "I just think we should check it out. After all, you're the primary on the Gant case."

Roulston squinted at the report again. "I don't know why I'm bothering, Houston, but just to humor you, I'll ask forensics to see what they can do with matching the bullet from Gant to this — what is it?" He pulled the report closer. "A Smith & Wesson model 422."

Stevie was relieved. She knew that without the actual murder weapon, the experts couldn't say definitively that the bullet had come from Kayson's gun, but through tests with the same model, they could confirm that it probably came from a Smith & Wesson model 422 — a .22 caliber target pistol.

"Can we go interview Kayson about it?"

Roulston paused, knowing he was falling into her trap. He was caught. Even though nobody, including him, gave a shit about a scumbag like Gant, he couldn't ignore a lead that could help him close this case. He liked to keep a high batting average, get his cases solved. He and Jovanowski were the heavy hitters on the squad, and with Jovanowski on the bench right now, it was his chance to shine. "All right. I'll go talk to him tomorrow."

"You mean I can't go?" Her disappointment was obvious.

"That's right. You're too caught up in this thing, Houston. You've lost your objectivity. Now why don't you go home for the night. Take a cold shower or something and leave Kayson to me."

*Like hell,* Stevie simmered, turning on her heel. She made a show of clearing off her desk and locking her gun away, then grabbed her jacket.

"G'night," she called to Roulston, who grunted back.

Stevie jogged downstairs to the second floor and hurried through the carpeted labyrinth to the area housing the drug squad. She was relieved to find her friend Pat at her desk.

"Hey, Stevie, what brings you down here? Christ, you'd think we worked at different ends of the city for all I ever see of you around this place."

Stevie shrugged. "They like to keep us probies hopping."

Pat's freckled face dimpled into a smile. "Fetching

a lot of coffee, huh? I remember, believe me. My probie days around here weren't that long ago."

Stevie smiled conspiratorially. Her friend Pat had no idea how deeply into this investigation she'd gotten herself, but she was in no mood to indulge at the moment.

"Listen, I need a favor. Can I use your computer?"

Pat shrugged broad shoulders. There weren't many women cops bigger than Stevie on the force, but Pat was one of them. "Sure, I was just leaving anyway. Your computers upstairs have gone down again?"

Stevie nodded a lie. "And I'm in a bit of a hurry."

"Help yourself."

Stevie waited until Pat disappeared down the hall, then switched the computer on. First she checked the national computer system, CPIC, to see if Kayson had a criminal record or was wanted anywhere else in Canada. Nothing. She tapped the keyboard again and plugged into OMPPAC. This would tell her if any police forces in Ontario had had dealings with him. Again, zilch. Kayson was clean.

She punched the keys with renewed vigor, her last resort the Metropolitan Toronto Police force's own computer network, in which its five thousand uniformed officers and nearly five hundred detectives filed their reports. Stevie tapped her foot impatiently, waiting for the information to appear. She knew the stolen gun report would be there, but if any of the city's officers had dealt with Kayson for anything else, even a speeding ticket, his name would come up.

Stevie's face clouded with each second. Finally,

the computer blinked twice, then blacked out. Dead as a doorknob. Stevie pounded the desk. "Fucking thing!"

A few minutes of pacing failed to bring the computer system back to life. After a fifteen-minute cup of cardboard coffee and plenty of steaming, Stevie returned. This time the computer fired up.

She punched in Kayson's name. There were two entries. First, the most recent, the stolen gun report. She scrolled down quickly until she came to the second one.

Her heart thudded wildly as she began to read, a smile slowly etching her face.

A neighbor of Kayson's had complained to police last summer about his bees. *Yes!* Stevie punched the air with her closed fist. Apparently, Kayson raised bees in his spare time, and a bunch had gotten away, thoroughly pissing off the ritzy neighborhood. Kayson got off with a warning, promising to move them to a more secure spot and to be more careful. Stevie hit the print button, brimming with confidence. So maybe she did have a hard-on for Kayson, but she was right about him, dammit! She'd make sure Roulston knew about this latest gem before he went to see the good bishop.

# CHAPTER THIRTEEN

Stevie had talked until exhaustion stole her voice. She'd told Jade all about the day's developments — searching Chiarelli's residence and finding the utensil drawer open ("He would have been looking for his needle kit after he was stung — that's why the drawer was left open. He would have been shocked to find it wasn't there!"); Kayson conveniently reporting his .22 stolen just weeks ago; and, finally, the discovery that Kayson raised bees in his spare time.

It felt good to share shop talk with someone, someone who mattered. She'd never had that luxury before. It had been so easy to bottle it all up — the crushed bodies at accident scenes, the drunks who puked and spat on her, the punks who called her names, the bar brawls, the women beaten black-and-blue by the men they kept going back to. Especially early in her career, Stevie would cry herself to sleep, silently telling Sarah about her day. Later, she didn't even do that. She'd simply numb herself with bourbon, trying to forget the ugliness.

"I talked to Teddy today."

"Hmmm," Stevie grunted, her head on Jade's lap, her eyes closed.

"He sounds a lot better. Should be out of the hospital in a couple of days. He was asking about you."

"Uh-huh."

Fingers began tenderly massaging Stevie's scalp. "Let's do something special tomorrow night, for our anniversary."

Stevie felt the sensation of floating in a warm pool of water, Jade's voice growing faint. The word *anniversary* repeated in her mind. "What are you talking about?"

Jade laughed. "It was a week ago tomorrow night!" Nothing from Stevie. "You *know,* that we first slept together."

Stevie nodded wearily, a slack smile on her face. "I gotta do something tomorrow night."

Jade's body stiffened. "Like work, I suppose? C'mon Stevie, all you think about is work. Can't you take a bloody night off?"

Stevie opened her eyes, bracing herself for the imminent tongue lashing. "I'm going to stake out Kayson."

147

"You're going to *what*?"

Stevie didn't answer, knowing perfectly well there was nothing wrong with Jade's hearing. She pushed herself up, rubbing the sleep from her eyes. "I've got to see what he's up to, Jade. Roulston won't end up doing dick with him. And after he pays him a visit tomorrow, Kayson might panic and do something stupid."

Jade stubbornly crossed her arms. "You can't do that alone. Aren't you supposed to work with partners or something?"

Stevie frowned. "I'm not even supposed to be on the McCleary case anymore. I'm doing it on my own time."

Jade stood now, hands on her hips, eyes black with anger. "What the hell are you trying to do, Stevie, get demoted? Or hurt? Or worse?"

Stevie shook her head as if to say Jade had no idea what the hell she was talking about, her voice condescending. "It'll be fine, Jade. I'm just going to watch him."

"Like hell. Maybe I'll give your inspector a call, see what he thinks of your plan."

Stevie leapt up, fists balled by her side, and shoved her flushed face into Jade's. "Don't you *fucking* dare. It's none of your goddamned business, Jade, so stay out!"

Jade's eyes widened in fear and bewilderment. Stevie, too enraged to notice, huffed away, grabbing her jacket from the post beside the door.

"You've got that fucking hero mentality, Stevie. That's what your problem is!"

"I'm sorry being with a cop is too much for you to stomach!" Stevie yelled back, slamming the door.

Stevie breathed hard in the elevator down, anger still bubbling through her veins. She'd seen other cops' wives or girlfriends, had a couple of uniform chasers herself come after her. Women were hot for the uniform, orgasmed over the power of it, but at the first hint of danger, they whimpered and withered. They couldn't take the heat, couldn't stay in for the long haul.

Stevie stewed on the drive home. She didn't need this shit, didn't need someone chaining her, worrying about her every minute she was working, making her second-guess herself. Fear had no place in a cop's mind. You reacted the way you were trained to. Fear, a cop's or loved one's, made you stop and think, made you waste precious seconds that could cost you your life in a dangerous situation. No way. Let Jade have some little doctor or nurse or accountant, someone who came home every night at the same time, safe and sound.

By the time Stevie got home and cracked open a bottle of bourbon, she'd begun to feel sorry for herself. Why couldn't anyone just love her for who she was? Why was *she* expected to change? Couldn't Jade be the one to change?

She swallowed another mouthful of fire, resisting the urge to cry, even when it began welling up in her throat. She'd been so damn sure about Jade, had felt so good about their love. Everything had felt so right, until tonight. She'd never felt this way about anyone before. She shrugged in the darkness and took another belt. It had been a good try, but what the hell. She liked being alone, was comfortable that way. It was all she knew, really. Hell, who had she been trying to kid anyway, thinking she could actually have a meaningful relationship with someone.

Stevie fell asleep in the chair, the bottle still cradled in her lap, tears dried hard and sticky on her face, tears she didn't even know she'd cried as drunken slumber took her.

Stevie propped her tired self up with coffee the next morning. Her whole body looked wrinkled and disheveled; her head ached. She tried to concentrate on paperwork as she waited for Roulston to return from his interview with Kayson.

A hollowness filled her gut, and it wasn't the hangover. Her fight with Jade had shaken her up more than she could admit.

Stevie found herself constantly wandering past her mail slot at the front of the squad room. A part of her hoped Jade would call. She even called her answering machine at home to check for messages. Nothing.

Inspector McLemore walked over and dropped a thick accordion file on her desk. "Stevenson trial starts next week. I want you to get up to speed on it and go to the courthouse every day in case the detectives need anything."

He quickly disappeared before he caught the scowl on Stevie's face. Obviously, he wasn't through humiliating her yet. He was keeping her on a short leash.

Stevie rubbed her throbbing temples. Nothing was turning out the way she'd expected. Not the homicide department and not her relationship with Jade. *Ex-relationship*. An empty sigh escaped her. *Dammit, it'd been good. No, great.* She'd never before thought it was possible for her, but it was. Or at least for a week it was. She wanted Jade back, wanted back what they had, there was no denying it. But she'd be damned if she'd go crawling back apologizing. It was Jade who had started it all, and if Jade couldn't learn to cut her some slack with her job, then it was pointless.

She looked up as Roulston walked in.

"How'd it go?" she asked anxiously.

Roulston shrugged, eyes averted in a look of boredom. "No big deal. He's not hiding anything as far as I can see."

"What are you talking about? What about the stolen gun?"

"What about it? It was stolen. It happens."

"And the bees?"

Another shrug. "He doesn't have 'em anymore. Got rid of them after the complaint was filed."

Stevie pursed her lips, her eyes narrowed cynically. He'd probably just moved the bees off his property to another location.

"So you took all this at face value, obviously," she grumbled acidly.

She saw the tightening in Roulston's jaw, the popped vein in his neck. He lowered his voice, not wanting to cause a scene. "Listen, Houston, I don't know who the fuck you think you are, but you're stepping way over the line here." His eyes hardened into a hateful glare. "The only reason you're in this department is because you've got a cunt. There's a lot of guys out there a hell of a lot more deserving than you. You should be working patrol, walking the Church and Wellesley beat. You'd like that, wouldn't you."

Roulston was smirking, his comment about Stevie enjoying working in Toronto's gay district meant to hurt her. "I've heard the rumors, Houston," he continued, whispering conspiratorially, a sly look on his craggy face. "You're into pussy, aren't you?"

Stevie glared back, her face expressionless.

"C'mon," he goaded her. "You can tell me. Hell, we can compare techniques."

"You're a ball-less fucker, you know that, Roulston?" Stevie said loud enough for everyone in the room to hear. "So concerned about what other people do in their bedrooms 'cause you can't get it up in your own? Huh?"

She stormed out, not giving a shit what her coworkers thought, not waiting for Roulston's reaction. She hastily took the stairs down and jogged out the main doors, anger following her like an insistent freight train. She found herself walking north up Yonge Street, maneuvering past the crowds of downtown shoppers and workers on lunch. She didn't feel the fat, lazy drops of cool rain soaking through her cardigan as her feet consumed block after block. She didn't feel the heavy leather shoulder holster and pistol cutting into her ribs as she strode on, looking purposeful, but feeling numb and directionless inside.

More than a dozen blocks later, she slumped down on a vacant bench inside a bus shelter. She knew now what she'd do. She'd keep an eye on

Kayson tonight, tomorrow night too, and that'd be it. If nothing happened, she swore, she'd let it go. But more than that, she decided right there on the spot, no matter what, today was going to be her last day in homicide. Come Monday morning, she'd march into McLemore's office and tell him she wanted out, wanted to go back to patrol. She didn't need all this shit from Roulston and McLemore. She wasn't going to be their footstool anymore. *Fuck 'em!*

Stevie began to shuffle back to headquarters slowly and wearily now. She was glad she'd reached a decision about their fucking candy-ass department.

Rain and sweat had completely soaked her, but she plodded on. She tried hard to ignore that damn hollowness tugging at her gut again.

# CHAPTER FOURTEEN

The macaroni and cheese dinner was about as tasty as a bowl of glue, but it would have to do. It was almost dark.

Stevie grabbed her leather jacket from the closet and stuffed her notepad in one pocket and a palm-size pair of binoculars in another. She'd already filled a thermos full of coffee. She was ready. She wouldn't have her gun — it was locked away at headquarters because, unlike police officers in the United States, she wasn't allowed to carry it off-duty.

It'd be all right. She was only going to watch Kayson, not confront him. She slipped into her ankle-high leather hiking boots and was about to tie them when there was a knock on the door.

It was Jade, huddling from the rain beneath her khaki trench coat. Stevie's mouth froze and her quivering knees threatened to buckle. God, how she wanted to pull Jade in and wrap her arms around her. The sight of Jade melted Stevie's heart, but not her pride.

"Can I come in?"

Stevie opened the door wider and stood aside. Jade stepped into the foyer, raindrops splashing onto Stevie's arm as she brushed past her.

Stevie leaned against the wall and crossed her arms over her chest. Definitely not the picture of contriteness. Her bravado made Jade want to laugh, for she knew it was all a silly facade.

"We need to talk, Stevie. I don't want it to end like this. In fact, I don't want it to end at all."

Stevie's guard collapsed in relief. She didn't think it was in her to make that first move, as Jade had just done. Jesus, what an idiot she was being. Why couldn't she ever say she was sorry? She felt her hands tremble and hugged them closer to her body.

Jade stared at her shoes before lifting her doelike green eyes — moist, imploring, fearful — to Stevie. "I'm sorry for worrying about you, Stevie. I shouldn't have jumped all over you the way I did. But I'm scared for you. I don't want anything to happen to you." Her hand moved to brush an intrusive tear from her face.

Stevie, who couldn't have considered anything

else, went to her and held her tightly, massaging the back of her head as Jade's wet face burrowed into her shoulder.

They stood, clutching each other. Stevie cupped Jade's glum face in her hands and kissed her lightly on the lips. "No, Jade, I was an idiot, flying off the handle like that. I'm not used to having someone around who cares for me so much." She wiped an errant tear from Jade's chin. "It just scares the hell out of me."

Jade nodded, her face brightening. "I know, Stevie, but I wish you'd tell me you're scared, or that I'm pushing too hard, instead of what happened."

Stevie hugged her again, knowing Jade was right, but less sure she could so easily change a lifetime of habits. "I'll try, Jade, I really will." She released her and went back to tying her boots, in a hurry to get going. "I'll make this up to you, I promise. As of Sunday, I'm dropping this whole Kayson thing anyway."

"And until then?"

"I have to do what I have to do."

"Then I'm going with you."

Stevie looked up from her task, astonished. "What?"

"I'm going with you, Stevie, so don't tell me I can't. Because if you do, I'll just follow you."

Stevie stood, exasperation screaming from every cell in her body, then pretended to bang her head against the wall in frustrated resignation. "Jade, this could be dangerous." She kept her cool, knowing full well Jade would do what she wanted to. "Why are you doing this? You can't be with me every time I go to work."

"I know that, Stevie, and I trust you that you'll be careful. But I have a bad feeling about tonight. I need to be with you."

Stevie slipped into her black leather jacket and pulled her black ball cap onto her head. She wasn't happy with Jade's intrusion into her work, but she wasn't about to risk another blowout with her. And besides, another pair of eyes couldn't hurt, especially since it was raining.

"All right then, let's go."

They decided to take Jade's car, a black Acura. It would blend in better than Stevie's convertible Mustang, and its windows were tinted darker.

Silence lingered like a heavy fog during the ride, Jade pondering her gut feelings and Stevie worrying about having an untrained partner, a civilian, along. Neither was happy with the arrangement, but both were resigned to its inevitability.

The rain cast a murky halo around the orange streetlights as Stevie pulled up to the curb, careful not to park directly under one of the lights. The neighborhood was posh: long wide manicured lawns, large colonial and Victorian style homes set well back from the street, expensive cars lining the circular driveways.

"What now?" Jade looked to Stevie.

"We sit and wait." Stevie took out her binoculars and scanned the grounds of Kayson's home. Lights were on inside, and no cars were in the driveway, but the garage door was shut. A computer search had already told her Kayson owned a dark red Ford Crown Victoria.

"You said you were going to be finished with this case Sunday," Jade waded into conversation. "Does that mean you're giving up?"

Stevie nodded slowly, as if not totally convinced herself. "I'm quitting the case and I'm leaving homicide."

Jade's jaw dropped. "Why? What's happened?"

Stevie shrugged. It was still too fresh to talk about. She was angry and hurt, and she wasn't in the mood for someone to try to talk her out of it.

Jade touched Stevie's forearm, then her hand fell on top of Stevie's. "Your decision or theirs?" she asked softly.

Stevie swallowed a dry lump. "Mine. I've had enough, that's all."

Jade stared ahead at the wet windshield, the raindrops dissolving into a blurred film. "They're making it tough for you, aren't they?"

"Something like that."

"I know what you're going through, Stevie." Jade searched Stevie's face, their hands still touching. "I went through a lot of shit in med school, and even more as a forensic pathologist. The old boys didn't exactly welcome me with open arms along the way. They don't do that with women, especially bicultural women, and dykes ... I might as well be a different species so far as they're concerned."

Stevie mentally kicked her self-absorption into the next hemisphere, suddenly guilty over how childish she was being. "I'm sorry, Jade." Her eyes probed Jade's; she felt triumphant for finally saying the words. She wanted to smile. "I've been acting like a total jerk the last few days. Can you forgive me? Can we just start over?"

Jade laughed, her eyes twinkling. "It's a deal, but you're not allowed to act like a jerk ever again, got it?"

Stevie saluted. "Got it, boss." She picked up the binoculars from her lap, still smiling, and raked the house. All was quiet.

"I wish you wouldn't quit homicide so soon, Stevie." Having thrown the match, Jade steeled herself for a flare-up. It really wasn't any of her business, but instinctively, she knew Stevie was too ambitious, too proud, to settle for an entire career as a patrol officer.

Stevie leaned back into the headrest, her voice low, her spirit fractured. "I've already decided."

"Can't you un-decide?"

Stevie suddenly laughed. "You just can't leave me alone, can you?"

Jade smiled, glad Stevie hadn't lashed out at her. "That's right. I won't leave you to wallow in self-pity or poutiness. It's just so unbecoming of a big tough cop."

She touched Stevie's cheek until Stevie turned to look at her. "You're good at your job, Stevie, too good maybe. You know you won't be happy writing traffic tickets and breaking up bar fights until you retire."

Stevie stared at her lover for what seemed like minutes, her face enigmatic. "Do you always have to be so damn right about everything?" Then she smiled, her voice playfully admonishing. "You won't even give me five minutes to pout and storm about, will you?"

Jade grinned and shook her head.

They shared the thermos of coffee, enjoying their time together and almost forgetting they had a job to do. They had never really just sat and talked for hours, and there was still so much they had to discover about each other.

They talked about their upbringings — Stevie's upper-middle-class roots out west, Jade's middle-class childhood in Montreal, the daughter of a stay-at-home mother and an architect father. Jade described her mother's embarrassment at having grown up on an Indian reserve, and confided how she'd refused to impart even a thread of that culture to her only child. She told how one rebellious summer as an adolescent, she paid a visit to long-lost relatives on the northern Ontario Ojibwa reserve her mother had shunned.

As the rain softly pelted the car, they even discovered that their birthdays were just three days apart, though Jade was six years older.

Stevie abruptly leaned over and kissed Jade's cheek.

"What's that for?"

"Just because I love you."

Jade smiled, her heart bursting at the seams, her arms itching to get Stevie home where she could really show her how much she loved her.

"Why did you get married?" Stevie suddenly asked, the question having nagged at her since they'd run into each other at the hospital right after Jovanowski's heart attack. She wanted to laugh at the silly image of Jade in a lacy white bridal gown.

Jade shrugged, embarrassment weighing down her

voice. "I was young and foolish — we both were. It was a pretty spontaneous thing. We were both in university and a little lonely, I guess."

"But why did you marry a man?" Stevie couldn't help her disapproving tone.

Jade shook her head and exhaled loudly. "I don't know. I'd had a couple of girlfriends, but I'd dated men too. At the time I thought I was bi. And I guess I thought I loved him. Unfortunately when I realized I didn't, I didn't end it. We hung on longer than we should have."

Stevie considered Jade's explanation, slowly swirling it around like a mouthful of virgin wine, exploring this new taste. This was a different Jade — one who, for once, didn't have all the answers, wasn't so surefooted. "Was he bitter?"

Jade shook her head again. "We both knew it wasn't right. We're still friends, and since he's a crown attorney, we still run into each other occasionally."

Stevie glanced at her watch. It was just past midnight. "Did you get married in a Catholic church?"

Jade snorted derisively. "Oh, yes. My family wouldn't have had it any other way. But I guess you could say I'm a black sheep in the Church now."

"Does your family know about you?"

"Yes, I've told them. They're okay about it, but my mom prays a lot for me, I suspect. What about you?"

Stevie hesitated, reticent to talk about her family. There were layers of pain there she wasn't ready to acknowledge, let alone work through. "I told them I was gay when I was nineteen," she finally answered, trying to sound flip. "I told them just to piss them off. Figured if they were going to treat me like I didn't exist, they might as well have a reason."

"And?"

Stevie shrugged. "Nothing changed. They pretended the whole conversation never happened. We just don't talk about it." She picked up the binoculars again, signaling an end to the topic. In her private moments, she'd always wondered if Sarah would have turned out gay as well. Probably not — she was the perfect child in everyone's eyes: extroverted, happy, affectionate, not introspective or sullen like little Stephanie. She probably would have grown up fulfilling everyone's expectations, and then some. But deep down, Stevie knew Sarah had loved her, had always tried to protect her, had never lorded over Stevie her place as the favored twin. She knew that if Sarah were alive today, she would love and accept Stevie as she was.

Just then Stevie noticed the automatic garage door opening. "I think Kayson's on the move," she uttered, stashing the binoculars away as the dark Ford began backing out of the driveway.

As the car approached them, Stevie quickly pulled Jade to her and kissed her passionately.

Watching the rearview mirror, Stevie waited until Kayson's car turned the corner before she started Jade's car and swung it around in a U-turn.

"Here we go," she muttered as she took off in pursuit. She was careful to stay about a block behind, which was easy to do since traffic was sparse.

Kayson weaved through the streets, heading south toward the lake, his route full of abrupt turns. Knowing the city like the back of her hand, a couple of times Stevie was able to take a parallel street, then zip across to pull in behind Kayson. So intent was she on following him, she didn't notice the same square headlights periodically popping up in her own rearview mirror.

"Are you scared?" she asked the silent Jade.

"A little," she answered cryptically.

Soon they were on the East Lakeshore Boulevard, zooming past the huge sewage treatment complex on the shore of Lake Ontario, Ashbridge's Bay looming as a dark mass on the right. Without signaling, Kayson abruptly turned right.

"Shit! He's going to Ashbridge's Bay Park," Stevie exclaimed.

She slowed, then flipped a switch to cut the headlights as she made the same turn. Kayson's glowing taillights looked like dual cigarettes in the distance. Then the tiny red dots disappeared altogether.

Stevie continued toward the lake, inching along slowly, her eyes peeled for Kayson's car. When she saw it, its lights off and parked near a patch of trees to her left, she turned right to put more distance between them. She stopped after about three hundred yards and killed the ignition.

"What do you think he's doing here?" Jade whispered.

Stevie squinted through the rain-blurred windshield, unable to tell whether Kayson was still in the car. "I'd say either he's going to do the world a favor and do himself in or he's here to dump something."

Stevie retrieved her binoculars. "Hold on, he's getting out of the car. He's opening the trunk."

"You think he might dump something over the seawall?" Jade offered.

Stevie watched as the tall, shadowy figure appeared to pull a large briefcase out of the trunk. "I'd say you're right on, honey."

"But we can't see the seawall from here. We need to get closer."

"I know," Stevie urgently whispered back, wishing Jade would quit echoing her thoughts. "You stay here and I'll see if I can follow on foot."

"No, he'll see you!" Jade hissed. "After this patch of trees, there's quite a stretch of open beach before you can even get to the seawall."

"You're right."

Jade reached behind her and grabbed a handful of old newspapers from the floor.

"What are you doing?" Stevie asked worriedly.

"He'll recognize you, but he won't recognize me." As she spoke, Jade grabbed the lapels of her trench coat and ripped with all her might, then did the same to her pockets.

"What the hell are you doing?" Stevie gasped.

Without explanation, Jade reached behind her head and pulled the elastic band from her hair, freeing it. With both hands, she mussed her long hair over her face.

"Jade, if you think —"

"I'll just keep an eye on him, Stevie. I'll lie on one of the benches like I'm some homeless person.

He won't even notice, and you can stay back in the trees." With the newspapers clutched in one hand, she grabbed the door handle with the other.

"I can't let you do this!" Stevie grabbed Jade's wrist in a viselike clamp.

Jade stared at Stevie. Her eyes, like dark stones, showed no signs of surrender. She yanked her wrist in the direction away from Stevie's thumb — the weakest part of a person's grip — and pulled free just as her other hand opened the car door. In a gust, she was gone, scampering away and stooping as she ran to pick up handfuls of mud, which she rubbed over her face and coat.

Stevie had to pick her mouth up off the floor mat. She'd been duped and even outmuscled by Jade. "Fuck!" she swore under her breath. If Jade got through this in one piece, she was going to damn well kill her!

Stevie slithered out of the car, by now having lost sight of both Kayson and Jade. Crawling along the soggy ground, she thought up names to call Jade. She directed her wrath inward, feeling ashamed and inadequate. How could she have let this happen? Her lover was out there in the dark with a man who had already killed three people. A five-foot, four-inch, hundred-and-twenty-five-pound woman would be a joke to him. *That motherfucker! I'll blow him away if he lays a single finger on her!*

Stevie groaned. Fuck! She didn't have her gun; she didn't have anything but her bare hands and a resolve as fierce as a battleship.

Jade crawled up onto the wooden bench at the edge of the tree patch, scattering the newspapers over her body as she curled into a ball, her arms covering most of her face. She could see the path before her. She heard his footsteps, the squishing of his shoes on the wet cement path. She stifled a sneeze as the scent of his cologne tickled her nostrils. She urged herself to be calm, to breathe steadily and evenly, as if she were sleeping. She held her breath as the shadowy figure walked past her. In her limited view, she saw his fist clutching the thick, hard-shelled briefcase. She emptied her lungs in relief. He had gone past without taking notice of her.

Jade propped herself up, her clothes a soggy mixture of rain and sweat, and peered over the back of the bench at Kayson striding on the beach toward the seawall, periodically turning his head to make sure no one was following him. Her heart was still galloping at the thought of how close she'd been to him as he walked past her — she could have reached out and grabbed him, or vice versa! Her chest tightened at the realization of how foolish she'd been, taking such a risk. She'd already lambasted Stevie for wanting to be a hero, for taking foolish risks, and now she'd been just as bad. Stevie was going to kill her.

She looked around, hoping Stevie would magically appear and pull her back into the trees. Then they could just drive off together, go back to Jade's and sip wine in front of the fireplace, and laugh at this whole foolish mess. But there was no Stevie, only darkness, and a killer disappearing into the foggy mist that had settled over the seawall.

Letting the damp newspapers float to the ground, Jade scrambled off the bench and, crouched low, ran toward the breakwall. It would have to be up to her to see what Kayson did with the briefcase. The window of opportunity was quickly closing.

Breathing hard, Jade squatted at the mouth of the seawall, the water lapping at the concrete. She was able to make out a figure standing at the end of it, hesitating. She heard the sound of a splash. Footsteps thudding on cement, gaining in tempo, drifted toward her.

*Shit!* There was nowhere to run except across the open beach before she could reach the safety of the trees. She was trapped.

She took a deep breath, knowing she had to either make a break for it or stay and be discovered. She darted off, not daring to look behind her, as her shoes dug into the soft, moist sand. The trees, like a waiting mother, grew closer and closer with each step. Her throat ached as her lungs insisted on more air. Then in one surreal instant she was airborne, her body horizontal, still driving toward the trees, before her face slapped the sand. She'd tripped. And even as her hands pulled up gloppy sand, clawing toward the protective bosom of the trees, a knee crashed into her back.

"Spying on me?" The voice was deep, educated, but gruff. Large hands roughly pulled her up by the shoulders. One arm clamped around her chest and the other painfully pinned her left arm behind her back.

"I don't know who you are, but you're obviously no friend of mine." His breath was warm on her neck as he pulled her backward toward the water again.

"Don't hurt her, Kayson! Just let her go!" It was

Stevie stepping out from the trees, slowly walking toward them.

The sickening prick of a knife jabbed Jade's left side, deflating any fortitude she might have still possessed. A tiny shriek escaped her lips, her legs quivering so badly that Kayson had to keep yanking her up.

"Fuck off, Wonder Woman!"

"C'mon, I know everything, Kayson. Harming her isn't going to accomplish anything."

Panicked, he changed direction and began dragging Jade along the beach, then toward the trees, but upwind of Stevie.

Stevie slowly followed. Kayson was taking Jade to his car. She knew she should bolt and cut them off before they got there, but she couldn't leave Jade alone with Kayson, stumbling and crying. If Jade lost sight of Stevie, she might totally fall apart and cause Kayson to finish her off right there.

"It's me you want, Kayson. I'm the better bargaining chip. Just leave her here."

"You'd like to call all the shots, wouldn't you? You think you've got everything all figured out," he yelled.

"I know you arranged McCleary's death," Stevie panted, a hollowness in her throat, her voice on automatic pilot. "Then you shot Gant because you knew he couldn't be trusted to keep his mouth shut. But that wasn't enough, was it? You had to take care of Chiarelli too, because he knew what you'd done, and you knew he was ready to talk about it. In fact, I'll bet Chiarelli initially approved of the idea of immobilizing McCleary in the archdiocese, getting his own parish out of it. But he couldn't quite buy into murder, could he?"

Kayson laughed wildly — a squeaky, high-pitched, ugly sound that prickled like a thousand daggers. "You think you know it all, don't you?"

Stevie gambled for more time. "That was pretty clever, what you did to Chiarelli. You brought those bees into the rectory in a food container, and let them out before you left, didn't you?"

Kayson, ignoring Stevie, grappled with Jade again. His grip slipped and she fell to the sand in a heap, unable, or unwilling, to get up. "Get up, damn you!" He kicked her hard in the ribs and ordered her up again, his voice low and breathy. He was on the edge.

At Jade's yelp, Stevie raced off at full tilt, rage constricting her throat and escaping in a guttural groan. It was as if she were catapulting through a tunnel, her eyes focused on her prey, her mind honed to the vengeful task at hand, her muscles rigid in anticipation.

Seeing her charge, Kayson desperately tried once more to haul Jade to her feet, but her trench coat ripped more as he pulled. His head jerked for a look in each direction, then he raised both hands high above his head as he sank to his knees over Jade's trembling form.

The glint of the knife halted Stevie in her tracks, her stomach caving in from an invisible kick. "Don't do it, Kayson!" she screamed desperately, the feeling of helplessness clutching her stomach. She had to swallow hard to keep herself from retching. The knife began its downward thrust, and she leapt again.

The crack of a gunshot echoed across the beach and was swallowed up by the water. Kayson dropped like a stone, splaying across Jade, the knife harmlessly spearing the sand.

No one moved for what seemed like days, the silence pregnant with the worst possibilities. Stevie crawled toward the heap of bodies. She reached Kayson first, his body motionless as it surrendered to death's tentacles. She scurried to Jade and pulled her out from under him.

"Stevie!" Jade cried weakly, reaching to touch Stevie's face.

"It's okay, love, just stay down. Someone's shot Kayson."

The figure moved out from the anonymity of the trees, the silhouette of a rifle in his hands.

"Stevie, Jade, are you all right?" He began walking toward them.

"Jovanowski?" Stevie squinted, disbelieving.

"Yeah, kid, it's me." He hovered over them, a lopsided smile on his chubby face. "Everybody all right?"

Stevie nodded, still dumbfounded. "How did you know?"

The veteran detective set the rifle down and knelt, placing a finger on Kayson's neck to check for the nonexistent pulse. Then he crooked a thumb at Jade. "Your buddy here phoned me today, told me about your ridiculous plans. We were worried."

Stevie hugged Jade closer to her. "You followed us?"

Jovanowski nodded smartly. "You see kid, ya still got some learnin' to do."

* * * * *

It was still drizzling later that morning as the police divers penetrated the cool water, dawn's emergence still fresh but too impotent to wash away the memories of what had happened on the beach just hours earlier.

Stevie glanced — couldn't look for long — at the spot where Kayson had nearly knifed Jade. The body had already been removed, but the images haunting Stevie weren't so easily carted away. She raised her hand to her mouth and clenched a knuckle between her teeth, hoping the pain would somehow dull the ache gnawing her insides. She could never have forgiven herself if she had lost Jade; if the loss itself had failed to destroy her, her own guilt would have.

Her mind reeled at how close, just seconds, she'd come to total destruction. She saw her whole life opened like a desert, rendered meaningless. If not for Jovanowski —

"You okay, Tex?" Jovanowski wrapped an arm around her.

Stevie nodded feebly. Her coworker would never know how much loss she'd been on the brink of. Or did he? Was that why he was being gentle with her?

"You know, we're going to have a lot of explaining to do. I'm just glad you and Jade are okay. Next time, though . . ." his voice trailed off.

"I know, Ted," Stevie whispered hoarsely. "Don't worry. There won't be a next time."

Stevie winced at the image of her whole career being flushed down the toilet. She had a lot of thinking to do, and hoping, and praying. Well, maybe

**171**

not praying. Still, whatever happened, she vowed to remain grateful that things hadn't turned out worse. Jade had suffered a cracked rib and plenty of bruises, but nothing a couple of weeks' rest wouldn't heal. She was tough. They both were, and they'd get through this, Stevie told herself hopefully.

"Detective Jovanowski, we've got something here," an officer in dark coveralls yelled from the seawall.

Stevie and Jovanowski headed toward the clustering of officers, where a spotlight had been rigged along with a canopy to keep the rain off. A gloved officer picked the locks on the dripping wet briefcase, then carefully opened it.

Inside lay a Smith & Wesson .22 handgun, a small plastic container, and a soggy leather-bound book with the word *Journal* stamped across it. Stevie bent over for a closer look since they couldn't touch anything yet. The label on the container warned that medicine was contained within.

"Chiarelli's epinephrine kit," Stevie nodded at Jovanowski. "And the journal. It's probably McCleary's. Kayson must have instructed Chiarelli to take it after Mrs. Powers discovered the body."

Her stomach loosened its nauseous grip. Whatever else her superiors said or decided about her fate, in spite of Kayson's lack of confession and his taunting laugh, she'd been right.

She remembered his final words: "You think you know it all." Then she smiled. Oh, yeah, she did have all the answers this time, and she didn't need his sick explanation or his macabre approval for unraveling his evil deeds.

\* \* \* \* \*

At home, a warm cup of coffee in her hand, Stevie paged through the damp journal belonging to Father McCleary. Near the end, she found a reference to Kayson. He'd called McCleary one day to inform him his former boyfriend Gant was living in the city, and not to have a repeat of the ugly incident twenty years ago.

Stevie closed the book. It must have been Kayson's way of planting the seed in McCleary's mind that another relationship was possible. Then Gant, at the instruction of Kayson, would have planned to run into McCleary in the gay ghetto in order to re-ignite the affair. The connection to Kayson in the diary would have been why it was taken by Chiarelli.

# CHAPTER FIFTEEN

Stevie smoothed a wrinkle in her silk white vest as Inspector McLemore motioned her into his office. She hadn't bothered to retrieve her pistol from her locker; she wasn't sure she'd even have a gun after this meeting.

McLemore, his face cryptic, mutely signaled for Stevie to take a seat across from his desk. The ubiquitous, stale smell of cigarettes hung in the air. She felt like standing, wanted to take it like a woman, but found herself obeying his command. Nervously, she drummed her fingers on her thigh and

174

took refuge in fixating on the shiny black leather of her square-toed cowboy boots.

Neither said anything for a moment, but she felt McLemore's eyes on her just as surely as she would have heard him screaming at her.

McLemore coughed. Stevie looked up.

"Look Stevie, I'm not going to kid-glove you. What happened over the weekend was reprehensible. I can't even begin to count the department violations you committed. For God's sake, you almost got a civilian killed, not to mention you risked your own life! And for Jovanowski, just barely out of the hospital I might add, to show up like the cavalry would be absolutely laughable if this weren't so deadly serious."

He waited for Stevie to respond. She counted the rhythm of his breathing. What the hell did he want her to say for crissakes? Did he want to nail her to the cross?

"Yes sir, I was a hundred percent wrong to do what I did. I understand that now. I foolishly let the case take control of me." She wasn't happy for giving in so easily but knew it was her only chance. *Okay, nail away.*

McLemore slowly shook his head. "You solved the case, Stevie, but at a tremendous expense. I want you to think seriously about whether you still want a career in policing, and if so, in what capacity."

Stevie stared at his tie — shades of blue, a pink cartoon caricature of the Pink Panther lurking in the middle of it. She would have laughed had she not felt like puking at this very instant.

She raised her eyes, gritted her molars, and decided to fight. She didn't deserve this — well,

175

maybe a shit-kicking, but not to be thrown out on the street. And they'd just love it for her to voluntarily resign. Then the whole ugly mess wouldn't have to reach the department's upper echelons, wouldn't have to leach into the press and embarrass the department. But she wasn't going to roll over and die. By god, she was going to prove her worth every day, prove they couldn't get by without her, that they'd be foolish to even think of letting her go.

"I want a career in policing, Inspector. And I want to remain in this department."

Mild surprise briefly ascended in his eyes, then narrowed to a tiny dot. "Why?"

Stevie cleared her throat, but her voice was forceful. "Because policing is the most important thing in the world to me. It's what I want to do. It's who I am. I'm good at it, sir, and I'm a good detective. I will be a great homicide detective if I'm given a second chance."

"And you think we should give you that second chance?"

Stevie didn't hesitate. "Yes. And this time I won't disappoint you. And I'll work within the rules, of that you can be sure."

McLemore studied her, gauged her sincerity, her intensity, her heart. He must have liked what he saw, for a small smile formed at the corners of his mouth.

"Jovanowski was in here earlier this morning. Said he'd go to the wall for you, no question. Said you're the best rookie dick he's ever seen, next to himself of course."

Stevie nodded. "The feeling's mutual, sir." Then her face colored. "About going to the wall, I mean."

McLemore's face was taut again, like a kite string in a stiff wind. "All right, Stevie, you can stay on. But you're suspended for two weeks. And your six-month probation in this department is extended to a year." He stood, indicating an end to the meeting, his face still grim.

Stevie got to her feet, relief liquefying her body, forcing her to grab the back of the chair for support. "Thank you, sir."

"By the way, I heard about that little episode with Roulston Friday. I've already spoken to him about it and now I'm speaking to you. Personal differences stay outside the office. We're not an effective team if we're at each other's throats. Got it?"

Stevie nodded, a huge grin ready to explode. She could hardly wait to tell Jade the news that she was staying on. Maybe now that they had a couple of weeks, they could take that drive north for a vacation. Then maybe they could come back and start house hunting!

"Stevie?"

"Oh, ah, yes, sir, of course."


Stevie followed behind and stood uncomfortably by while first Jovanowski, then Jade, stopped just inside the entranceway, dipped a finger into a silver receptacle containing holy water, then blessed themselves. She awkwardly scampered into the pew ahead of them while they paused to genuflect, then watched curiously as they dropped to their knees for a moment of silent prayer. She felt foolish for her ignorance of the customs and habits of Catholicism, then quickly felt foolish for feeling foolish in the first place.

She had twisted Jade's arm to get her to come with her to St. Mary's, ditto for Jovanowski. Both claimed to be recovering Catholics, yet their church etiquette was as polished as the most dutiful. *Funny how old habits die hard.*

The organist began playing in earnest, cueing the congregation to stand and sing a hymn that everyone but Stevie seemed to know the words to. She glanced nervously around. No one was watching her.

The procession floated up the center aisle — robes swishing, a wooden cross held high, altar boys and girls leading, following. Then Stevie caught sight of him — Father Peter LaRoche. His head held high, shoulders squared, eyes straight ahead, he let the coterie carry him to the altar, which he kissed upon his arrival. It was almost untraceable, but not to Stevie; she saw the shadow of a grin, and like a ray of sunshine after a horrendous storm, she let it pierce her until it soon filled her with a reverence that was majestic in capacity. Not reverence for him so much, not reverence for the church or religion, but at all that was good and right and hopeful.

Stevie glanced up at the stained glass windows and the cathedral ceiling. It was all his now, Father Peter LaRoche's. She smiled, rubbing her shoulder against Jade's. All the ugliness here was over now, of that she was sure.

Then her gaze was pulled to the altar, where

Father LaRoche presided. His first words: "Welcome, my brothers and sisters. In the name of the Father, and of the Son, and of the Holy Spirit."

Everyone crossed themselves in unison.

"Let today be a new beginning for our church, for our community, for all of us as individuals."

A few of the publications of
**THE NAIAD PRESS, INC.**
P.O. Box 10543  •  Tallahassee, Florida 32302
Phone (904) 539-5965
Toll-Free Order Number: 1-800-533-1973
*Mail orders welcome. Please include 15% postage.*
*Write or call for our free catalog which also features an*
*incredible selection of lesbian videos.*

LAST RITES by Tracey Richardson. 192 pp. 1st Stevie Houston
mystery. ISBN 1-56280-164-3 $11.95

EMBRACE IN MOTION by Karin Kallmaker. 256 pp. A whirlwind
love affair. ISBN 1-56280-165-1 11.95

HOT CHECK by Peggy J. Herring. 192 pp. Will workaholic Alice
fall for guitarist Ricky? ISBN 1-56280-163-5 11.95

OLD TIES by Saxon Bennett. 176 pp. Can Cleo surrender to a
passionate new love? ISBN 1-56280-159-7 11.95

LOVE ON THE LINE by Laura DeHart Young. 176 pp. Will Stef win Kay's
heart? ISBN 1-56280-162-7 $11.95

DEVIL'S LEG CROSSING by Kaye Davis. 192 pp. 1st Maris Middleton
mystery. ISBN 1-56280-158-9 11.95

COSTA BRAVA by Marta Balletbo Coll. 144 pp. Read the book,
see the movie! ISBN 1-56280-153-8 11.95

MEETING MAGDALENE & OTHER STORIES by
Marilyn Freeman. 144 pp. Read the book, see the movie!
ISBN 1-56280-170-8 11.95

SECOND FIDDLE by Kate Calloway. 208 pp. P.I. Cassidy James'
second case. ISBN 1-56280-169-6 11.95

LAUREL by Isabel Miller. 128 pp. By the author of the beloved
*Patience and Sarah.* ISBN 1-56280-146-5 10.95

LOVE OR MONEY by Jackie Calhoun. 240 pp. The romance of
real life. ISBN 1-56280-147-3 10.95

SMOKE AND MIRRORS by Pat Welch. 224 pp. 5th Helen Black
Mystery. ISBN 1-56280-143-0 10.95

DANCING IN THE DARK edited by Barbara Grier & Christine
Cassidy. 272 pp. Erotic love stories by Naiad Press authors.
ISBN 1-56280-144-9 14.95

TIME AND TIME AGAIN by Catherine Ennis. 176 pp. Passionate
love affair. ISBN 1-56280-145-7 10.95

PAXTON COURT by Diane Salvatore. 256 pp. Erotic and wickedly funny contemporary tale about the business of learning to live together. ISBN 1-56280-114-7   10.95

INNER CIRCLE by Claire McNab. 208 pp. 8th Carol Ashton Mystery. ISBN 1-56280-135-X   10.95

LESBIAN SEX: AN ORAL HISTORY by Susan Johnson. 240 pp. Need we say more? ISBN 1-56280-142-2   14.95

BABY, IT'S COLD by Jaye Maiman. 256 pp. 5th Robin Miller Mystery. ISBN 1-56280-141-4   19.95

WILD THINGS by Karin Kallmaker. 240 pp. By the undisputed mistress of lesbian romance. ISBN 1-56280-139-2   10.95

THE GIRL NEXT DOOR by Mindy Kaplan. 208 pp. Just what you'd expect. ISBN 1-56280-140-6   11.95

NOW AND THEN by Penny Hayes. 240 pp. Romance on the westward journey. ISBN 1-56280-121-X   11.95

HEART ON FIRE by Diana Simmonds. 176 pp. The romantic and erotic rival of *Curious Wine*. ISBN 1-56280-152-X   11.95

DEATH AT LAVENDER BAY by Lauren Wright Douglas. 208 pp. 1st Allison O'Neil Mystery. ISBN 1-56280-085-X   11.95

YES I SAID YES I WILL by Judith McDaniel. 272 pp. Hot romance by famous author. ISBN 1-56280-138-4   11.95

FORBIDDEN FIRES by Margaret C. Anderson. Edited by Mathilda Hills. 176 pp. Famous author's "unpublished" Lesbian romance. ISBN 1-56280-123-6   21.95

SIDE TRACKS by Teresa Stores. 160 pp. Gender-bending Lesbians on the road. ISBN 1-56280-122-8   10.95

HOODED MURDER by Annette Van Dyke. 176 pp. 1st Jessie Batelle Mystery. ISBN 1-56280-134-1   10.95

WILDWOOD FLOWERS by Julia Watts. 208 pp. Hilarious and heart-warming tale of true love. ISBN 1-56280-127-9   10.95

NEVER SAY NEVER by Linda Hill. 224 pp. Rule #1: Never get involved with . . . ISBN 1-56280-126-0   10.95

THE SEARCH by Melanie McAllester. 240 pp. Exciting top cop Tenny Mendoza case. ISBN 1-56280-150-3   10.95

THE WISH LIST by Saxon Bennett. 192 pp. Romance through the years. ISBN 1-56280-125-2   10.95

FIRST IMPRESSIONS by Kate Calloway. 208 pp. P.I. Cassidy James' first case. ISBN 1-56280-133-3   10.95

OUT OF THE NIGHT by Kris Bruyer. 192 pp. Spine-tingling thriller. ISBN 1-56280-120-1   10.95

NORTHERN BLUE by Tracey Richardson. 224 pp. Police recruits Miki & Miranda — passion in the line of fire. ISBN 1-56280-118-X   10.95

LOVE'S HARVEST by Peggy J. Herring. 176 pp. by the author of
*Once More With Feeling.* ISBN 1-56280-117-1    10.95

THE COLOR OF WINTER by Lisa Shapiro. 208 pp. Romantic
love beyond your wildest dreams. ISBN 1-56280-116-3    10.95

FAMILY SECRETS by Laura DeHart Young. 208 pp. Enthralling
romance and suspense. ISBN 1-56280-119-8    10.95

INLAND PASSAGE by Jane Rule. 288 pp. Tales exploring conven-
tional & unconventional relationships. ISBN 0-930044-56-8    10.95

DOUBLE BLUFF by Claire McNab. 208 pp. 7th Carol Ashton
Mystery. ISBN 1-56280-096-5    10.95

BAR GIRLS by Lauran Hoffman. 176 pp. See the movie, read
the book! ISBN 1-56280-115-5    10.95

THE FIRST TIME EVER edited by Barbara Grier & Christine
Cassidy. 272 pp. Love stories by Naiad Press authors.
ISBN 1-56280-086-8    14.95

MISS PETTIBONE AND MISS McGRAW by Brenda Weathers.
208 pp. A charming ghostly love story. ISBN 1-56280-151-1    10.95

CHANGES by Jackie Calhoun. 208 pp. Involved romance and
relationships. ISBN 1-56280-083-3    10.95

FAIR PLAY by Rose Beecham. 256 pp. 3rd Amanda Valentine
Mystery. ISBN 1-56280-081-7    10.95

PAYBACK by Celia Cohen. 176 pp. A gripping thriller of romance,
revenge and betrayal. ISBN 1-56280-084-1    10.95

THE BEACH AFFAIR by Barbara Johnson. 224 pp. Sizzling
summer romance/mystery/intrigue. ISBN 1-56280-090-6    10.95

GETTING THERE by Robbi Sommers. 192 pp. Nobody does it
like Robbi! ISBN 1-56280-099-X    10.95

FINAL CUT by Lisa Haddock. 208 pp. 2nd Carmen Ramirez
Mystery. ISBN 1-56280-088-4    10.95

FLASHPOINT by Katherine V. Forrest. 256 pp. A Lesbian
blockbuster! ISBN 1-56280-079-5    11.95

CLAIRE OF THE MOON by Nicole Conn. Audio Book —Read
by Marianne Hyatt. ISBN 1-56280-113-9    16.95

FOR LOVE AND FOR LIFE: INTIMATE PORTRAITS OF
LESBIAN COUPLES by Susan Johnson. 224 pp.
ISBN 1-56280-091-4    14.95

DEVOTION by Mindy Kaplan. 192 pp. See the movie — read
the book! ISBN 1-56280-093-0    10.95

SOMEONE TO WATCH by Jaye Maiman. 272 pp. 4th Robin
Miller Mystery. ISBN 1-56280-095-7    10.95

GREENER THAN GRASS by Jennifer Fulton. 208 pp. A young
woman — a stranger in her bed. ISBN 1-56280-092-2    10.95

TRAVELS WITH DIANA HUNTER by Regine Sands. Erotic
lesbian romp. Audio Book (2 cassettes)     ISBN 1-56280-107-4     16.95

CABIN FEVER by Carol Schmidt. 256 pp. Sizzling suspense
and passion.                               ISBN 1-56280-089-1     10.95

THERE WILL BE NO GOODBYES by Laura DeHart Young. 192
pp. Romantic love, strength, and friendship.     ISBN 1-56280-103-1     10.95

FAULTLINE by Sheila Ortiz Taylor. 144 pp. Joyous comic
lesbian novel.                             ISBN 1-56280-108-2      9.95

OPEN HOUSE by Pat Welch. 176 pp. 4th Helen Black Mystery.
                                           ISBN 1-56280-102-3     10.95

ONCE MORE WITH FEELING by Peggy J. Herring. 240 pp.
Lighthearted, loving romantic adventure.   ISBN 1-56280-089-2     11.95

FOREVER by Evelyn Kennedy. 224 pp. Passionate romance — love
overcoming all obstacles.                  ISBN 1-56280-094-9     10.95

WHISPERS by Kris Bruyer. 176 pp. Romantic ghost story
                                           ISBN 1-56280-082-5     10.95

NIGHT SONGS by Penny Mickelbury. 224 pp. 2nd Gianna Maglione
Mystery.                                   ISBN 1-56280-097-3     10.95

GETTING TO THE POINT by Teresa Stores. 256 pp. Classic
southern Lesbian novel.                    ISBN 1-56280-100-7     10.95

PAINTED MOON by Karin Kallmaker. 224 pp. Delicious
Kallmaker romance.                         ISBN 1-56280-075-2     11.95

THE MYSTERIOUS NAIAD edited by Katherine V. Forrest &
Barbara Grier. 320 pp. Love stories by Naiad Press authors.
                                           ISBN 1-56280-074-4     14.95

DAUGHTERS OF A CORAL DAWN by Katherine V. Forrest.
240 pp. Tenth Anniversay Edition.          ISBN 1-56280-104-X     11.95

BODY GUARD by Claire McNab. 208 pp. 6th Carol Ashton
Mystery.                                   ISBN 1-56280-073-6     11.95

CACTUS LOVE by Lee Lynch. 192 pp. Stories by the beloved
storyteller.                               ISBN 1-56280-071-X      9.95

SECOND GUESS by Rose Beecham. 216 pp. 2nd Amanda Valentine
Mystery.                                   ISBN 1-56280-069-8      9.95

A RAGE OF MAIDENS by Lauren Wright Douglas. 240 pp. 6th Caitlin
Reece Mystery.                             ISBN 1-56280-068-X     10.95

TRIPLE EXPOSURE by Jackie Calhoun. 224 pp. Romantic drama
involving many characters.                 ISBN 1-56280-067-1     10.95

UP, UP AND AWAY by Catherine Ennis. 192 pp. Delightful
romance.                                   ISBN 1-56280-065-5     11.95

PERSONAL ADS by Robbi Sommers. 176 pp. Sizzling short
stories.                                   ISBN 1-56280-059-0     11.95

CROSSWORDS by Penny Sumner. 256 pp. 2nd Victoria Cross
Mystery.                                    ISBN 1-56280-064-7      9.95

SWEET CHERRY WINE by Carol Schmidt. 224 pp. A novel of
suspense.                                   ISBN 1-56280-063-9      9.95

CERTAIN SMILES by Dorothy Tell. 160 pp. Erotic short stories.
                                            ISBN 1-56280-066-3      9.95

EDITED OUT by Lisa Haddock. 224 pp. 1st Carmen Ramirez
Mystery.                                    ISBN 1-56280-077-9      9.95

WEDNESDAY NIGHTS by Camarin Grae. 288 pp. Sexy
adventure.                                  ISBN 1-56280-060-4     10.95

SMOKEY O by Celia Cohen. 176 pp. Relationships on the
playing field.                             ISBN 1-56280-057-4      9.95

KATHLEEN O'DONALD by Penny Hayes. 256 pp. Rose and
Kathleen find each other and employment in 1909 NYC.
                                            ISBN 1-56280-070-1      9.95

STAYING HOME by Elisabeth Nonas. 256 pp. Molly and Alix
want a baby . . . or do they?              ISBN 1-56280-076-0     10.95

TRUE LOVE by Jennifer Fulton. 240 pp. Six lesbians searching
for love in all the "right" places.       ISBN 1-56280-035-3     10.95

KEEPING SECRETS by Penny Mickelbury. 208 pp. 1st Gianna
Maglione Mystery.                           ISBN 1-56280-052-3      9.95

THE ROMANTIC NAIAD edited by Katherine V. Forrest &
Barbara Grier. 336 pp. Love stories by Naiad Press authors.
                                            ISBN 1-56280-054-X     14.95

UNDER MY SKIN by Jaye Maiman. 336 pp. 3rd Robin Miller
Mystery.                                    ISBN 1-56280-049-3.    10.95

CAR POOL by Karin Kallmaker. 272pp. Lesbians on wheels
and then some!                              ISBN 1-56280-048-5     10.95

NOT TELLING MOTHER: STORIES FROM A LIFE by Diane
Salvatore. 176 pp. Her 3rd novel.          ISBN 1-56280-044-2      9.95

GOBLIN MARKET by Lauren Wright Douglas. 240pp. 5th Caitlin
Reece Mystery.                              ISBN 1-56280-047-7     10.95

LONG GOODBYES by Nikki Baker. 256 pp. 3rd Virginia Kelly
Mystery.                                    ISBN 1-56280-042-6      9.95

These are just a few of the many Naiad Press titles — we are the oldest and
largest lesbian/feminist publishing company in the world. We also offer an
enormous selection of lesbian video products. Please request a complete
catalog. We offer personal service; we encourage and welcome direct mail
orders from individuals who have limited access to bookstores carrying our
publications.